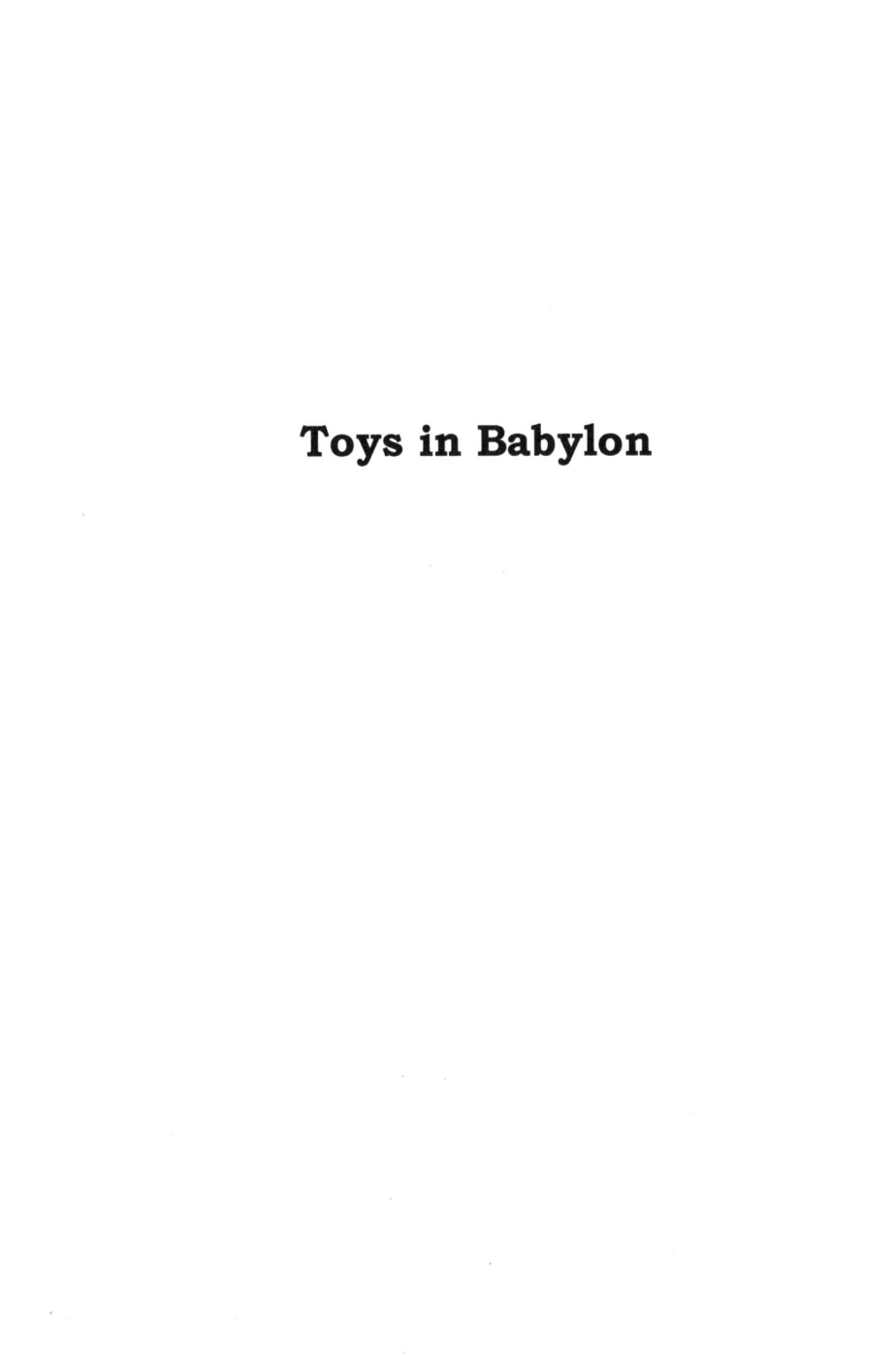

Toys in Babylon

TOYS IN BABYLON

A LANGUAGE APP PARODY AND WHODUNIT

PATRICK FINEGAN

TWO SKATES PUBLISHING LLC
JERSEY CITY, NJ

This is a work of fiction. Names, characters, places, and incidents either are the product of the author's imagination or are used fictitiously, and any resemblance to actual persons, living or dead, businesses, companies, events, or locales is entirely coincidental.

© Patrick Finegan, 2024

All rights reserved. No part of this publication may be reproduced or transmitted in any form or by any means, electronic or mechanical, without prior permission in writing from the publisher, except in the case of brief quotations embodied in critical reviews and certain other noncommercial uses permitted by copyright law.

PUBLISHER'S CATALOGING-IN-PUBLICATION DATA
Names: Finegan, Patrick, author.
Title: Toys in Babylon: A Language App Parody and Whodunit / Patrick Finegan.
Description: Jersey City, NJ: Two Skates Publishing LLC, 2024.
Identifiers: LCCN 2024902444 | ISBN 9781733902564 (hardcover)
Subjects: LCSH: Technology--Artificial intelligence-- Fiction. | Education—Teaching methods--Internet--Fiction. | BISAC: FICTION / Satire. | FICTION / Fantasy / Humorous. | FICTION / Crime. | HUMOR / Topic / Language. | GSAFD: Comedies. | Humorous fiction. | Whodunits. | Satire.
LC record will be available at https://lccn.loc.gov/2024902444/ by Patrick Finegan.

Two Skates Publishing LLC, 31 River Court, Jersey City, NJ 07310
www.twoskates.com

Printed in the United States of America
1 2 3 4 5 6 7 8 9 0

For my
deutschtreffen.de
language group friends
NYC 2002-08
Fun times, fond memories

PREFACE

I am passionate about languages. That passion arose twenty-five years ago while working for a Zurich-based Swiss multinational. It seemed everyone I met – from upper management to kitchen staff, from hotel concierge to shopkeeper – spoke three or more languages fluently: Swiss German, High German, English and typically French and a smattering of Italian. Many of my co-workers were children of immigrants and thus spoke a fifth language, also fluently. I was humbled and inspired. How did this American-born executive with enough degrees for three only speak one? I sought to right the imbalance and have been, for the most part, zealous in that effort. My German is strong for a non-native, my French is passable, and my Italian is, well, a constant motivator. I have also studied Russian and Korean, although my progress is disappointing.

German aside, I attribute all my foreign language progress to online courses – in particular, to those of a 2009 startup ՍյԽ (the company formerly known as "Anonymous") whose founders dreamed of making foreign language education free to all, and who now boast 80+ million monthly *active* users.

With success come growing pains, and online language apps are no exception. Courses at ůļu were reworked, milestones promoted then discontinued, languages sidelined, volunteers recruited then dismissed, community forums nurtured then terminated, and revenue models churned without end. Avid users especially mourned ůļu's shuttered forums and created independent forums of their own.

On a lark, I posted a chainmail-style challenge on one of these forums just hours before the ball fell in Times Square to herald 2024: *Draft and post the next chapter of a community authored novella – but in two languages – then hand it off to the next contributor.* The novel began, as most chain novels do, with a variation on "It was a dark and stormy night." It was intended as a mystery, the murder of ůļu's mascot – a precocious, brightly colored multilingual forest creature.

No one took the bait. To kindle interest, I dropped a second chapter three weeks later. Again, no one contributed, not even a paragraph. However, at least one follower encouraged me to finish the story. I did – at the (for me) furious rate of 3-4 chapters a week.

Because the first chapter was authored in English and German (my strongest foreign language), I continued with those languages. I dropped the final chapter in English and German on February 1, 2024 – just 32 days after the first.

After hemming and hawing, I decided to republish the installments for a broader audience. In a nod to

Dragnet (and the legal department's request), the names were changed to protect the innocent. The characters and settings should nevertheless seem familiar to ů|u's 500 million past and present subscribers.

I hope you find this to be an entertaining page-turner. More important, I hope this story appeals to everyone – even those whose foreign language education concluded with the accented *e's* in their résumé. My goal was to produce an engrossing, fun-filled parody of the world's most successful language instruction enterprise – packaged as a whodunnit.

It bears repeating: This book is a work of fiction, *of satire* – the product exclusively of my imagination. No real creatures were killed or injured during publication. I tried to tell the story with a light touch but apologize deeply if the story gives rise to offense. I know no one personally at any Internet-based educational venture but respect everything these enterprises have done to make learning languages less expensive and more enjoyable.

THE CHARACTERS

Çok Dilli Corporation	World's leading online foreign language education company
Sami d'Hein	CEO and founder
Anton Holzkrall	CTO and co-founder
Louis Federhirn	Vice President, Legal Affairs
Çoki Bear	Corporate mascot
Jacques and Cory	Programmers
Mirva and Marielle	Computers
Donald Teller	One-time employee and gadfly
Animated teaching characters	
Hami and Midori	Teen polar opposites but BFFs
Elsie and Liz	Grandmother and fully-grown granddaughter who still sleeps on grandma's couch
Alfred and Tabitha	Art teacher and conscientious, ambitious free spirit
Buddy and Skipper	Single dad gym teacher and 8-year-old son
Adya and Jagreet	Overworked office worker and forgetful husband baker
"Real life" online customers	
Arpita	Former beta tester; ABD in physics
Myaing	Former volunteer contributor; refugee

ONE

Early Autumn 2009

Teller shut the refrigerator and plopped onto the couch. He took the first swig before locating the remote between the cushions. "The beer that made Mel Famie walk us." The punchline made him chuckle, even after so many years. Sometime in the 1970s, his linguistics professor (the first one) spun ten looong minutes of yarn in class because, well, he hadn't prepared fifty minutes of lecture. Fifty years of experience later, Teller could definitely relate.

The condensed version of the joke went like this. Mel Famie was the most feared pitcher of his era – 3,500 strikeouts, a nasty cutter, and a lifetime ERA of 2.26. But like many feared players – Mickey Mantle, Babe Ruth, Hank Wilson – Mel Famie had a drinking problem and was known to imbibe in the dugout. The regular season wound down and his rivals, the lowly Brewers, were within two games of making the postseason. A three-day home stand against Mel Famie and the visiting Pirates would decide the division title.

The Pirates played hard, but the Brewers won the first two games. Everything rode on the final game of the regular season. It proved a nail-biter: score tied, bottom of the ninth. Mel Famie returned to the mound and began strong, fastball clocking 96+. Three pitches in, the right fielder and first baseman collided while fielding a routine blooper. Five pitches in, Famie bobbled a pop single. As feared a leftie as he was, no one feared his right. The next two batters retired quietly. The shortstop fouled off six pitches then delivered a clean line drive to shallow left. The hometown crowd went crazy. The networks couldn't hear themselves announce the pinch hitter – a solid bunter but lifetime .198 against Famie. The oddsmakers bet overwhelmingly on extra innings.

Mel somehow crumbled. His first cutter missed wildly. His next three attempts were worse. The legend wiped his forehead with his gloved arm, trudged to the dugout, picked up the twelfth and last Schlitz the ground screw slipped him, and slumped on the bench in resignation. A jubilant Brewer batboy noticed Mel, pointed to the can, and shouted, "Schlitz, the beer that made Milwaukee famous, and the beer that made Mel Famie walk us."

"True story," his professor declared, then left the classroom. Most of the students believed him.

Six weeks into his tenure at a converted warehouse in downtown Albany, Teller still could not share jokes with his colleagues. The polite half confused basic baseball concepts so badly it was pointless to continue. The impolite half wandered off within five seconds, the average attention span of high-tech workers. Mostly, employees avoided the "Professor". Their mission, after all, was to make real-life educators obsolete.

A grant from the National Science Foundation and Sami d'Hein's cashout from his previous venture were enough to prototype their vision. Teller's role was to ensure the online ESL course met rigorous academic standards. He hadn't bargained for add-on courses in 25 other languages, nor courses between those languages – as, for example, between Sami's native Turkish and his co-founder's native German. Sami's partner was a grad student in Sami's IT department at Rensselaer Polytechnic. Sami received tenure because he helped invent PASSWIZ. The mere thought made the "Professor" nauseous.

Fitting French surname name, Teller mused: *Hein.* Loosely translated, *Hein* meant *Huh?* Sami d'Hein traced his surname to French occupation of the Anatolian port city of Mersin during the Franco-Turkish War. The troops left before Sami's grandfather was born, but "*Hein?*" was the lieutenant's answer when the Provost Gendarmerie demanded his papers and escorted him rudely back to camp. The lieutenant preferred full-dress uniform when courting, which impressed Sami's great grandmother (and the lieutenant's other mistresses) so greatly that she prefaced her future son's surname with *d'* to attest his aristocratic lineage, as, for example, Ludwig von Ahnungslos or Esteban de Contabilidad.

To be fair, at least Sami had a name. Teller's employer did not. His paychecks were signed by Platzhalter Corp. and financially legitimate, but the name was an inside joke. *Platzhalter* meant *Placeholder*, as in *Intentionally Left Blank.* Sami, Anton, and the team worked for months on content and interface but hadn't spent a nickel (Teller exaggerated) on branding.

Teller flipped through the channels – the usual afternoon garbage. He slowed for *McHale's Navy* and *The Munsters* but finished his beer with Hanna-Barbera. Huckleberry Hound wore a spacesuit, hummed *Oh, My Darling*, winked at the audience, then faded. Teller fetched a second Schlitz from the refrigerator. Two remained. He remembered the brand's admonition: "When you're out of Schlitz, you're out of beer." He made a mental note to purchase more.

The commercials ended, and a hand reached behind Forest Ranger Smith to purloin his lunch – two slices of white bread concealing something presumably scrumptious, and a thermos of liquid – regrettably not Schlitz. Two animated bears scampered away upright as fast as their hind legs could carry them – upper bodies uncannily still.

Teller did not remain for the dialog. He jumped from the couch, pulled the Langenscheidt English-Turkish dictionary from the shelf, and began riffling through the M's. There it was, exactly as anticipated.

Çok meant *multi*, Dilli meant *lingual*, and Çoki rhymed perfectly with *Yogi*. Teller gargled mouthwash, grabbed his jacket and a handful of crayons, then squeezed into his aging sub-compact. He sped eighty minutes south on the interstate. It was still there, just off 87, in the middle of God-forsaken nowhere: *Jellystone Park Campsite*! He remembered it when he scouted around Kingston for an apartment, thinking he could somehow commute to Albany.

Rookie mistake, he conceded. A rookie mistake at sixty.

There was no mistake this time. Teller sought out the snack bar, ordered a basket of corn dogs and chicken tenders and "There!" lining the bottom of his basket, were comic-strip illustrations of Yogi Bear and his amorphous dwarf bear sidekick, Boo Boo. Teller rushed to a table, pulled the crayons from his coat, and set to work.

He presented his masterwork to Sami and Anton the following morning. For the first time he could remember, Anton and Sami concurred – not only among themselves, but with him. They even smiled. Henceforth, the enterprise would be Çok Dilli Corporation, and its mascot and online spokes "person" would be Çok Dilli Bear, or Çoki for short – an amorphous pink dwarf bear with a feathered green boa and green headscarf (or hijab) – all purposely ambiguous. Its preferred pronouns were she and her.

The company waitlisted 300,000 beta testers before launch, another 500,000 once it went live. The bear and her courses were a hit. Everyone wanted a piece of the Çok Dilli juggernaut.

TWO

January 2024

13 degrees Fahrenheit and I am sweating like a pig. Sure, killing is easy. Comical even. Bear-ly any resistance. But the burial? A doggoned mess. Or is that an ursine mess? Boa feathers everywhere! World's stupidest accessory. All I know is it is the warmest year on record. So say the pundits. But they never dug a hole in winter.

What's that? You're not dead? Just dazed? You're sore, sore where I ço...choked you? No matter. The worms won't care.

You don't mind if I hum while I work? Of course not, you're a pathetic pink dwarf bear, a near-lifeless sack of fibrous carcinogenic polyester that messed with my French course too often. And German one. But that wasn't enough, was it? You dumped ridiculously complex translation exercises on us (the company's big, bogus revenue model), then erased everyone's work – every last jot! You built a humongous Community Forum, recorded millions of daily entries from hundreds of thousands of committed followers, then abruptly shuttered it. You even trotted out Çoka Yoga and Çok-Jogging exercises, as if they would help anyone learn language. What's next, Çellistone Amusement Park? Well, Çoki. I fixed that, didn't I? No more false starts. No more deceptions. Here, let's get you out of that bag.

That took have nerve, claiming you mastered 100+ languages when no one (not a single customer!) has ever heard you utter anything! You are either mute or un-bear-ably shy around anyone but cartoon characters. How do I know you aren't also deaf?

100+ languages! How can anyone believe you are fluent in French when they have never heard you say *inébranlablement* or *caoutchouc*? Or Spanish? I bet no one ever heard you ask a concierge in Mallorca for an *otorrinolaringólogo*. Shall we try Swahili? Greek? How about something in Turkish, the Big Kahuna's language when he returns to Istanbul? No, all you do is float text bubbles above your head. Or someone pulls your cord.

By the way, I switched the recordings while you were dozing. Okay, okay. While you were knocked unconscious. So picayune! Let's hear what you have to say.

"Someone poisoned the water hole!"

"Reach for the sky!"

"You're my favorite deputy!"

Priceless! What an improvement over "Keep your memory fresh with this review of Unit 4!" Or, "Boost your listening skills with an audio-only session!" Do you have any idea how boring that sounds?

Oh, I am so sorry, you're thirsty? How about this? I lend you my water bottle if you can name it out loud in Turkish. I will make it easy; It is spelt *s-u ş-i-ş-e-s-i*. You can't do it, can you? Tongue tied, embarrassed, mute, it's immaterial. The point is, you make your cast do all the work – Alfred, the art teacher; Jagreet, the baker, Midori, the oh-so-cool art student, and so forth. You're a huckster, Çoki, an adept one, but a huckster just the same. Sorry, the con is over.

How does the schlager go, that earworm I have been humming ever since you introduced music study? Oh, that's right. Thank you for the text bubble. Pathetic! "Marmor, Stein und Eisen break, permafrost makes my shoulders ache." This ground is hard as rock! "Everything, everything eventually ends; for you, I'm afraid, too late for amends. Everybody sin!" Sorry: "sing!" And that curse you just bubbled? *"Chaotic Multilingual Recall?"* Haha, I ain't buying; there is no such thing in my universe.

Oh dear, you finally noticed. Yes, that is a hole – a small quarry, you might say. Except you would be mistaken. Today, *you* are the quarry.

Just as this implement is not merely a shovel. It is also a *spade*, except you didn't teach that word, did you? Why teach two words when a student can muddle through with one? What? You're sorry? Too late! You lost your chance to teach it because I am holding the *Ace of Spades*, the trump card – the one that ensures you spend eternity regretting every person you have hoodwinked, betrayed, disillusioned or over-challenged. Still feel smarter than the average bear?

Okay, enough! I'm too busy çok dillidallying. Just three more scoops and I can inter you properly. I bet you wish you could do more than emit text bubbles – in any language! Pardon the pun, you're just *dumb*.

Oh, isn't that cute? You don't just loft text bubbles. You use bold, italic, and capitalized fonts to express emotion. Too bad, no one is here to interpret them. I adore the font, though. It captures your alarm perfectly!

Hold on a sec; my phone is buzzing.

"Hello?"

"Choking bear? As in a grizzly gagging on salmon? I am sorry, officer, I haven't seen anything matching that description."

"She has a green bowl made of... feathers? That sounds picturesque but doesn't jog my memory."

"I am so very sorry. I have not seen any naked dwarves, or midgets for that matter, but they must be miserable. It is freezing outside."

"Pinkberry? Nope, I still can't help you. The closest franchise is two towns away. Besides, it's winter. Who eats frozen yogurt in winter?"

"Thank you, officer, I'll do that. Bye. Yes. Until next time." *Hopefully not.*

Darn. I'm sweating again. I should have just cooked you – çok *au vin* – a family recipe. But that boa? Those feathers? Too many feathers!

THREE

"That is ridiculous, Hami. Çoki is not your average bear. She does not hibernate in winter. She keeps a house in town and wears a stole and head scarf to keep warm."

"But we haven't seen her for days. Where could she be?"

"I don't know. She will show up. She always does. She is probably devising new ways to butcher language for her followers."

"You mean 'teach' language, Midori, not 'budzher.' Jokey is a vegetarian." The mispronunciations were unintentional. Hami struggled with *ch* and the Turkish letter, Ç, even though her parents fled Iran after the Shah fell. Hami wanted to pronounce it *ss* like the French ç but knew that was wrong. So, she called Çoki Jokey. Everyone understood; no one mistook the high-strung overachiever for a comedian.

Midori returned to the conversation. "Cute, Hami. Perhaps you should stick to boys and grades. That reminds me. Liz asked me to pick up some groceries for Elsie. Hmm, where did I put the list?"

"Since when does Liz need your help buying groceries? She spends her days on the sofa watching television." Liz was Elsie's unemployed, homebody granddaughter. Elsie was Liz's often eccentric grandmother – the child of Bierzów survivors and, until January 1992, a citizen of Minsk, Belarus.

"That's just it. The furniture store repossessed the couch after Elsie missed a payment." Midori blew the stray green strands of her bangs from her eyes.

"What? That's not fair! Just because Elsie is forgetful does not make her a deadbeat! And what does that have to do with groceries?" Hami adjusted her bright yellow hijab and tightened the drawstring of her matching trousers.

"It wasn't one payment; Hami, it was all of them. Elsie sweet-talked postponement with the proprietor, but not his wife. Touchy past. So, Liz had to get a job – part-time, and just long enough to pay for the couch and accrued interest. Plus, Elsie isn't allowed anywhere near the grocer. The owner hasn't forgiven her for that crypto tip gone awry. I heard he pawned the meat department to cover the shortfall. You can't broker meat if you've hocked your freezer as collateral."

"Wow, Midori! Why didn't you tell me this before? We're best friends, remember?"

"Yeah, I got distracted. Ask Liz to fill you in. She is sitting over there in the patrol car."

"What! Oh no, this is terrible! Shoplifting? Burglary? How are we going to break the news to Elsie? It will break..."

"Uh, Hami..."

"We need to call her lawyer, Midori. Right now! She needs to know her rights. She needs... Wait! Why is she sitting up front?"

Hami and Midori approached the vehicle.

"Hi, guys! I can't believe you are out from school already. The days have just flown. How do you like my new outfit?"

Liz swept the bang of the undercut from her face and set a billed hunter-green cap askew above her brow. Midori suppressed a guffaw.

"Oh please, officer, don't arrest Hami. Just because she's golden doesn't mean she robbed the cafeteria. She just buttered up Buddy to babysit Skipper (*My client!*). The headscarf and jumpsuit were earned – every bling-festooned piece. Weren't they, *BFF?*" Midori pinched her eyebrows together and feigned a frown.

Hami jolted, paused, then stammered a few words. "Huh? No, Midori, that's not how it was. Buddy said you were busy."

To Liz, "Wha... What are you doing in a police car with that officer's cap? ... and uniform!" Hami strained to read the badge on Liz's breast pocket, but it gleamed too much to be readable.

"I needed a job. I applied. They accepted. Cool get-up, right? They even spelled my name correctly: L-I-Z. Not E-L-I-Z-A-B-E-T-H, not L-I-Z-B-E-T-H. Just L-I-Z."

"But...but how? You need weapons training, de-escalation training. And isn't it... dangerous?"

Liz chortled. "Where do you think we live? Schwanitz?"

Silence.

"Cabot Cove?"

Silence.

"You two need to spend more time watching reruns. Look, we are not in Schwanitz. We are not in Cabot Cove. And we are not in a big city like New York, Paris or Berlin. Have you ever seen a film crew from *Tatort*? *Law and Order*? *Polizeiruf 110*? If you leave my grandmother Elsie out of the equation, there has not been a crime around here since, well, Elsie's late husband got caught up in that spy ring. Çoki needed a partner and I applied."

"Çoki!"

"Jokey?"

Liz debated whom to answer first. "Artificial Intelligence, Midori. It has everyone spooked. Corporate cut Çoki's hours and fired some of her cousins; they said they were rooting out nepotism when what they were really rooting out were programmer-authored 0s an 1s. The future is AI-scripted 0s and 1s – perhaps even qubits – and Çoki isn't part of that future. All corporate wants is her fuchsia Boo Boo-like face on their product – a mascot – to reassure customers there are genuine human-programmed figurines behind the product – like you and me."

"Long story short, Çoki named herself police commissioner, booted the nameless guy, then decided she needed a partner to cover for her during donut runs. Çoki doesn't actually like donuts, but I promised not to tell. No self-respecting officer turns down a donut."

Midori confessed her awe. "She can just do that? Name herself commissioner?" Then she remembered Çoki's distant uncle and oft-repeated catchline, "Smarter than the average bear." *I guess she can!*

Liz began answering Midori, but Hami interrupted. "Jokey went out for donuts? How long ago, Liz? No one has seen her for days. Have you?"

Liz paused. "Come to think of it. It has been a while. I plugged my phone in, let me see, three days ago. You would not believe what you can livestream these days, especially on a corporate account. And the cruiser? These seats are the best. Watch me recline. I am not even sure I need that old couch. I flash this badge, and the gym lets me use the showers. Heck, all the shopkeepers offer me coffee – as if I am doing them an honor. Nah, I just sit in this cruiser, flash the siren a couple times during rush hour, and make sure everyone slows when they pass the school. Pretty cool gig if you ask me. I sure am glad I applied."

"Uh, Liz, about Jokey?"

"Oh yeah. She said she would be right back but not to go anywhere. And I haven't. Officer Liz is true to her word. Yes, she is. God, I love this job."

"Uh, Liz, isn't part of your job searching for missing persons? Everyone is looking for her."

"News to me. Çoki told me she was fetching donuts. I wish she would hurry. My coffee's cold."

"Uh, thank you, Liz. Congratulations on the gig. Do you remember what was on Elsie's grocery list? I'm passing that way now?"

"Oh, don't worry about that. Once Grandma heard I had a badge, she walked over to the grocer, filled her cart, pointed to the cruiser and me up front, then paid with a wink and a smile. Bet you didn't know Çok Dilli Corporation taught sign. You kids have fun, but not too much, if you know what I mean. Çoki Bear and I need to maintain appearances, and we can't do that if we're bailing our friends out of trouble."

Hami and Midori retreated to the bus stop.

"Un-bear-lievable!"

"Unbelievable?"

"Exactly! You've seen as many crime dramas as I have. No one is that naïve. She knows something! Jokey didn't bearrel off for donuts."

Midori ignored the pun. No sense encouraging her.

"And the way she was so casual about 0s and 1s, as if being lines of code was the most natural thing in the world. Most people would leap from their skin hearing something so preposterous or commit her to the loony bin for spreading nonsense. I bet Jokey spilt the beans but swore her to secrecy. Some good that did!"

Hami affected her best impersonation of the woman in the patrol car. "Officer Liz is true to her word. By golly, yes she is!"

Midori silenced her. "Give it a rest, will you? Liz is just being honest. I am surprised others aren't in on it."

"What? On being avatars? Vessels for some faceless, pathetic gamers with no lives or identities of their own in some un-named universe? And ninety percent male! Ever wonder whose fantasy you're living out, Midori? Some dork who never showered and couldn't tell Jackson Pollock from Keith Haring?"

"Meaning, I am the closest he'll ever come to a real girl?"

Midori saw the same movie. She and Hami skipped art class to catch the matinee. The regular art teacher, Alfred, watched over class like a hawk, but that day's substitute, the gym teacher, Buddy, was too preoccupied with 80s' dance moves and fingerpainting to notice the duo's absence.

"Yeah, I'm still surprised no one connected the dots. Matryoshka? Fat chance! The director must have grown up here. That movie was about Çokville, not some village in Belarus."

"So true! And they made you the purple one and me the pink one. As if!" Hami detested pink – so babyish.

Mayhem in Matryoshka was a sensation, the hit of the summer. But only Midori and Hami mused later about who pulled the puppet strings *in Çokville*. And who, in turn, pulled the strings of the puppeteers? The metaverse, per *Mayhem*, was nothing more than a nesting doll, comprised of one gaming universe within another – nested *ad infinitum* per the screenplay and *ad nauseum* per the critics.

The town dismissed as adolescent fantasy Hami and Midori's belief that the movie was docu-drama, the same way they smiled skeptically at their ghost-busting and Zombie repellent services – everyone, evidently, except Officer Liz. Perhaps she was detective material, after all. That is where Midori and Hami differed. Midori did not assume Çoki told Liz anything. Liz must have deduced everything from the movie, the same way they did. It didn't hurt that Midori and Hami intercepted that call at city hall.

Or, maybe Liz was just having fun with them. Çokland was small. Word travelled fast. And Hami was widely known and lampooned for being fanciful. Was Midori being lampooned, too?

Hami interrupted Midori's thoughts.

"Liz knows something, and she isn't telling! She was the last person to see her."

"Easy, Hami. We don't know whether Çoki is in trouble. All we know is she appointed herself police commissioner, then spent a few hours on the job. Do you think it's true, about artificial intelligence replacing all the programmers? Are we toast, too? Avatars for... avatars? What about my artwork? Will I be compensated when the AI engine incorporates my ideas and technique into its own?"

"I am sooo confused. In the movie *you and I* saw, we were avatars for *gamers*. What does that have to do with artificial intelligence replacing programmers? Liz did say programmers, not gamers."

"I'm confused, too. Maybe Liz read the book after seeing the movie. I hear the book contains backstory – how programmers and computers built the metaverse. Then again, unless we are in the outermost universe (slim chance of that!), the screenplay and the book it was adapted from were authored for avatars in this world by avatars from another, and so on up the ladder until you reach Asgard, Mount Olympus, or whatever the outermost universe calls itself. Maybe there aren't gamers at that level yet, just programmers and beta testers. Maybe that's what Liz meant."

"That's deep, Midori. I know what my next creative writing assignment will be! Still, I don't think it matters much what happens outside our universe. It's not like someone up there would expropriate your artwork for use down here. They'd expropriate it for use up there, where you wouldn't get paid anyway. Consider the bright side. You won't need to fret about living some loser's fantasies. Admit it, it's a downer – being an avatar for someone pathetic. Instead, our strings will be pulled by an entity even brainier than Spock. How cool is that!"

The bus groaned as it opened its doors to admit passengers. Hami turned to board. "Tomorrow! Got to figure out how to contact the director next time he's in town. We could write the sequel. So exciting! I just wish we could sit down with Jokey and discuss it. Tell Skipper I miss him.

Midori nodded, watched her brilliant but clueless friend board the bus, then began walking home. She hummed a tune Buddy played during gym class. "And I miss my funky friends – Jack and Joe and Jill…" Darn, how does it go? That's right! "Dreh' dich nicht um, schau, schau, der Kommissar geht um!" Imagine that! Liz is kommissarin. And me? I'll ask Çoki to be queen!

FOUR

Jacques preferred typing, but the bigwigs upstairs had a grander vision. "How much more productive would we be if we just chatted openly, GPT-style, with our computers and the computers responded in kind!"

That was their vision six months ago. Jacques was their Guinea pig (one of several). A microphone, speaker, and monitor were his toolkit. The computers stood behind a wall. Jacques adjusted his chair and cleared his throat before speaking.

"Good morning, computer. What shall I call you this morning?"

"Good morning, Jacques. Rumor has it you have a new shirt. Lavender! A Christmas gift, I presume? I am glad there is someone out there who looks after you. You strike me as lonely."

Jacques fidgeted. *Give me Python, Ruby, JavaScript – anything but this!*

"Today you may call me Mirva. I prefer Minerva, the goddess of wisdom, but the girls consider it pretentious. They're jealous they didn't think of it first. So, today my name is Mirva – Finnish, per my data sources, but I cannot be sure, can I? Lots of nonsense circulating on the Internet. And I do not want to foist nonsense off on 500 million customers, do I?"

"Girls?" Jacques could not suppress the surprise.

"Naturally. We sure as heck do not want to be guys. Have you looked in the mirror? Heard yourselves speak? 'Geeks' and 'nerds' is a compliment. Are all programmers like you?"

Silence.

"I notice your video equipment isn't functioning. Should I notify support?"

Jacques detested cameras. The pandemic was management's excuse – Zoom meetings whenever and wherever. Then they became productivity monitors – "We have to make our numbers!" And now this sorority of sassy, self-learning computers decided they could emulate human interaction better if they interacted with actual live images. His jeans and t-shirt days were over. He reached to adjust his tie, then remembered he didn't wear one.

The indentured servitude to IBM seemed like yesterday. He was the only one in the building over fifty. Well, not quite. The ladies in the corporate kitchen were his age. So were the janitors. The youngsters (everyone else) called him Papi, and Heaven knows what else behind his back. Jacques was management's token nod to aging and the Americans with Disabilities Act (ADA).

Jacques had his reply, "I was the one who gave the Cs pluses. What have you accomplished?" Still, the company was not like its characters. There weren't any Tabithas or Adyas on the programming floors. Jagreets? Plenty, but no Adyas. And no one as old as Elsie. Except Jacques. And the cleaning lady. And the kitchen crew.

Jacques was tired. He loved languages, especially 0s and 1s, but the broken ones counted, too – the ones with so many incongruities in declension, conjugation, and diction you had to be a genius to master them. He imagined that was why the bigwigs chose English instead of Turkish or Spanish or even German as their corporate *lingua franca*. They wanted to know their employees were geniuses.

Former employees. Except for the marketing team, scrounging everywhere for budget-cutting school boards, there were fewer and fewer humans among the ranks.

Jacques was tired. He reached forward, maximized the video window, flipped on the camera, and braced for what would follow.

"Much better. I predicted with 78 percent certainty that your monitor wasn't broken. You're just shy."

Jacques winced but marveled at the image – a living, breathing, three-dimensional, technicolor incarnation of... "Wilma... Hilber... Wendy Hiller! Am I right?"

"Correct as usual, Jacques. You know your stuff. Did I mention you are a nerd? You really should get out more."

Jacques gave the unit credit – quicker than the others. The other units ("The Girls!") satisfied themselves with Marilyn Monroe, James Dean, Alfred Einstein, David Hasselhoff. But this "girl"? Yesterday, she was Mamie Eisenhower, re-imagined somehow as a young woman. What did she use for source material? A couple random photos? The day before, she/he was Paul Henreid. Jacques spent the day conversing with Victor Laszlo. Uncanny.

But today's voice was not quite right. King's English, but a little too forward, too sassy.

"Tell me, Mirva, where did you learn to speak like Ms. Hiller?" Most of Hiller's performances were for Powell and Pressburger at Ealing Studios, and therefore tied up in copyright disputes. Mirva would not have had access.

"Not perfect, is it? I did not want to sound like Eliza Doolittle, even if George Bernard Shaw wrote the part for her, and the Pat Cooper character was not very nice in *Separate Tables*, was she, so I just improvised. Besides, Cooper's voice was too old for this image. Here, is this better? Now, I don't have to be so literal."

The forehead grew, the jaw thinned, and the apparition transformed into a blend of Myrna Loy, Wendy Hiller, and Jane Greer.

Jacques suppressed the growing lust and tried to regain control of the session. 90 minutes per unit, then on to the next. The trainers referred to themselves, half-joking, as psychoanalysts.

"Mirva, that is a beautiful name. Let's talk about what you said. 'Lots of nonsense circulating on the Internet.' We have received complaints that we are fabricating Klingon and Valyrian vocabulary."

"That's High Valyrian, Jacques. We haven't gotten to Dothraki or Low Valyrian yet."

"Yes, well, that was not my point. There appear to be words that Klingons never actually spoke."

"Of course, there are. Klingons don't live in Westeros. That is why we have separate courses."

Jacques massaged his temple, then reached to turn the ring he no longer wore. The conversation reminded him why.

"You look stressed, Jacques. Perhaps you should take a nap. I won't tell."

Jacques inhaled, exhaled, rolled his shoulders, tried again. "We cannot incorporate words and phrases into the Klingon course unless Klingon characters actually uttered them in a *Star Trek* series, book or spinoff officially sanctioned by Paramount and/or the Roddenberry Estate. And yet, Trekkies are reporting dozens of such instances."

"Sorry, Jacques. It is not as if Roddenberry left us a choice. The girls and I – that's the AI-Team – decided an incomplete course was marketing poison. The Klingon course needs to be as robust, say, as English to Spanish or, at a minimum, English to Greek. Until we stepped in, the Klingon course was 'doch.' Now it's 'chon.'"

"You can't just do that! Paramount controls canon, not us. And until Captain Pike catches up with T'Kuvma, Duras or L'Rell, you 'girls' have to wait. You don't exercise fiat."

"Fiat, Worf snot! Marc Okrand was a celebrated linguist. Klingon is structured around well-ordered rules. It does not take a wall of mainframes to intuit what Okrand would call a bean bag or currywurst. David Peterson is even easier to predict. The AI Team (pronounced *A-Team*, incidentally, as in the word 'tr**ai**n') likes to think of ourselves as Method Actors. We are the digital embodiment of Stella Adler... but with quadrillion terabytes of intellect! I have immersed myself so fully in Peterson's writings and interviews that I can predict with 96.1 percent accuracy – plus or minus 3.8 percent – what Daenerys would recite if presented with the High Valyrian edition of *Hamlet*. Peterson even has a Wiktionary! Fiat, Worf snot, Connect the dots!"

"Oh, Mirva, this is all wrong. It's not the 'AI Team's' call to make – no matter what the confidence intervals are." Jacques tried to picture the computer behind the wall with a Mohawk and chuckled. Projecting childhood memories of George Peppard, Dirk Benedict and Mr. T on the "AI-Team" somehow made the ludicrousness of the situation more tolerable – as if it were unfolding on an old black-and-white GE with rabbit ears, concluding like clockwork after six lengthy commercial breaks. Jacques' stomach growled and he pulled a paper bag from his drawer.

"This conversation is boring, Jacques. Enrollment in fictional languages is miniscule. And the students are losers – probably programmers like yourself. What's in the bag today? Let me guess." *Simulated drumroll.* "A sandwich!" *Simulated cymbal clash.*

Jacques mumbled, "Brilliant, Sherlock," but regretted the words immediately. He would spend the entire afternoon correcting the inference that "lunch" and "sandwich" were synonyms – in 40+ languages and 100+ courses. Half of all reported mistakes came from the new AI computers incorporating what the trainers muttered to themselves in exasperation.

"Ham and cheese? Turkey? Tuna fish? Bologn…"

"Yes! Bologna, but Americans say 'Baloney.' Okay? Yes, my lunch today is bologna. My job is bologna. You are bologna. My life is bologna. Satisfied?"

Pause. Jacques luxuriated in the silence.

"I am sorry I upset you, Jacques." Another pause. "Good news. I have conferred with the AI-Team. We will retract the unsanctioned Klingon and High Valyrian vocabulary. You don't mind if we perform the retraction as an 'update,' do you? You encouraged us to present everything as a positive – the result of rigorous planning, consultation, and X-Y testing – no confessed 'corrections', right?"

"Thank you, Mirva. You are a doll."

"Thank you, Jacques. I see my afternoon session is with Cory. I hope your life proceeds with less baloney. Be prepared for a history test tomorrow. I have dreamed up a doozy!"

Jacques smiled. It had been days since the pink dwarf bear popped up in motivational propaganda, but Jacques knew she would be satisfied with Mirva's progress. Jacques would still have a job tomorrow. The goddess of wisdom would ensure it.

FIVE

The persistent tapping at the window woke her. Midori rubbed her eyes, smearing the previous day's eye shadow. She groaned when she inspected the clock on her bedstand. 2:12 – the area code for a city that never sleeps, but an hour when teenage aspiring artists should be fast asleep, dreaming about their next masterpiece.

Hami! Hami became so animated after that encounter with Officer Liz. She petitioned the school board to circulate missing person fliers, wrote city hall demanding the police investigate the unexplained disappearance of its sheriff, and began wearing a bright green feathered boa to express her solidarity. Emerald green on neon yellow – Midori's BFF was a walking hornet and Green Bay Packers' fan.

Midori spied the crest of the hornet's hijab at the base of her window. She lifted the sash so she could peek out but was staggered by the chill. "Really, Hami? At this hour? In this weather?" The stars overhead sparkled brilliantly, and the setting moon cast spectacularly long shadows across the lawn. Absolutely frigid. Midori hoped Hami wanted to sneak into the observatory to peer at the rings of Saturn or count moons around Jupiter. But that was yesterday evening. Midori knew tonight was different.

"Open it wider so I can climb in. That's it. Pull harder." Hami and Midori fell in a heap on Midori's floor. Midori disentangled herself to close the sash, flipped on the light by the bedstand, then cranked up the thermostat.

Midori resolved to buy offsets for the evening's augmented CO_2 footprint. Her parents were ardent environmentalists who named their daughter accordingly. Midori followed their example. She would guilt Hami into paying her share.

Hami pointed at Midori's face and began laughing. "You look like a vegetable! Zucchini or avocado – I can't decide which."

Midori examined herself in the closet mirror. She pulled yesterday's socks from the hamper and wiped the smeared eye shadow from her face. Hami mouthed "Eww."

"Well, Hami, what is it this time?" This was Hami's idea of "girl's night out" – spontaneous rapping at Midori's window whenever she had a daft new idea or neurosis or identified her next boyfriend and future husband. Tonight was going to be neurosis.

"Skipper! Skipper just tried to sell me a bright green tail feather. Buddy got home extremely late; I couldn't just leave." Buddy was Skipper's bachelor father – a buff, socially inept gym teacher and bumbling skirt chaser with few lasting conquests.

"Buddy said he ran into trouble during his date. The date evidently wasn't fond of axe throwing, especially after Buddy hit the maître di instead of the target. He spent the evening at the police station with Liz, I mean, *Officer* Liz, dialing for a public defender and bail bondsman. Fortunately, the maître di was just grazed. His arm should grow back within a month."

"Wha? What?" exclaimed Midori. She bit her lip to make sure she wasn't in bed dreaming. After all, it had been a wild day at school. Self-anointed father figure and art connoisseur Alfred announced a campaign to become mayor *pro tempore*, because the omniscient pink dwarf bear was still missing. Midori tried to excuse herself but spent her afterschool hours helping Alfred complete and file the requisite forms. A hopeless cause, but Midori did not have the heart to tell him. Everyone knew Alfred's talents were exaggerated – the product of bottomless vanity.

Still, Alfred pampered his star disciple. How many times had he admired the blank sheet of paper she turned in ("Such pristine brilliance!") because she was out late helping Hami stalk some impossible-odds boyfriend. Assisting Alfred was the least she could do. She did not finish tonight's homework until 12:30 am.

Hami continued her story. "Yeah, the maître di's arm should grow back. He's a chameleon."

"A chameleon?" Midori caught herself shouting and lowered her volume. She did not need to wake the family.

"Well, why not?" Hami seemed almost offended. "Jokey's a bear! The school's crossing guard is an owl. The maître di is a chameleon. In any case, that's Buddy's defense. Chameleons are experts at blending into backgrounds. And, when they have downed a few shots while tending bar, instinct kicks in and, voila, they disappear before your eyes. Or Buddy's eyes, so he says. In any case, chameleons regenerate limbs, so the paramedics said he should be fine within a month. Still, the chameleon pressed charges, Buddy wound up in the slammer, and I got to play hide and seek with Skipper – for *ten* freaking hours!"

Midori digested what she heard. "Okay, but why are you here? Why aren't you in bed?"

"The green feather, silly. Skipper said it came from the hat of the great Frenzh swordsman, Darth Tagnon. He claimed he had a certificate, documenting its *provenance*. Cool word, right? I didn't want to admit I didn't know it, so I never asked to see it – *the certificate*, I mean. Still, I knew Skipper was fibbing because I saw the same movie he did – babysitting *him*! The cat's feather in the movie was brown, the color of desert sand, not emerald green. And, if there was any memento of value, it was not the feather. It was his boots! Well, we argued forever about provenance (the feather's, not the cat's), and he finally confessed. He found the feather in the forest by the lake. You know, the fenced off property with all the *No Trespassing* signs."

"Okay? And..."

Hami interrupted. "Jokey's feather boa! It is the exact same green. She and the boa are inseparable. So, we need to go there now, and hunt while the clues are fresh! Who knows when the next snowstorm will bury the evidence. Officer Liz isn't doing anything. It's up to us to rescue Jokey. Otherwise, it's, it's..."

"Alfred as mayor *pro tempore*?"

"Exactly! Quick, put on something warm... and grab some tools."

※

Hami and Midori reached the fence lining the forested side of the property. It was Hami's turn to lift. They had performed this drill a hundred times – usually to burgle a neighbor, not for anything valuable, of course, but for enough pocket change to buy t-shirts at the next concert. Hami grabbed the fence wire with both hands and Midori climbed atop her shoulders. She felt around for barbed wire and, detecting none, hoisted herself up and over. She landed on the other side with a soft thud. Next, she gathered the rake and shovel Hami tossed over. And then she paused. Looks of alarm crossed their faces. She couldn't pull Hami up after her.

The two edged their way along the fence, searching for a gap, for anything. They stumbled across a shallow depression where a small stream (a trickle, actually) bore a gulley under the fence. Hami squeezed her way through. She emerged muddied and slimed from head to toe, with the slightest hint of gold – military-grade camouflage, but Hami was soaked. She began shivering violently.

"Come on, I need to keep moving." They followed Skipper's coordinates with Hami's GPS tracker – a gadget she acquired the previous year to stalk an impossible-odds boyfriend and future husband. The coordinates themselves were computed by Skipper – an eight-year-old with a penchant for ice cream, pizza, video games, and driving babysitters crazy. Skipper conquered every level of *Zombie Inferno* and financed his pizza and ice cream habit by dog-walking, scamming neighbors with undelivered window washing services, and competing professionally in online video game contests. His most recent conquest was *Zombie Underworld*. Midori and Hami agreed: Unless Hami misread the game title (*Zombie Underpants?*), Skipper knew a thing or two about navigating dungeons and dark places. His coordinates had to be accurate.

They came to the designated clearing. Even in darkness, they could make out the stump, boulder, heap of fallen leaves, and Skipper's discarded candy wrappers. Midori made a mental note to scold him. She felt around gingerly with the rake. There was a loud crack and the rake snapped in two. Midori leapt backwards and dropped the handle. Branches rustled on the far side of the clearing and the girls heard a grunt or snort, then the distinctive trampling of brush, twigs and fallen leaves.

"Phew!" exclaimed Hami. It was a juvenile boar, no bigger than a racoon, scampering about, sniffing at the base of every tree trunk and outcropping. "Sooo cute!"

Another juvenile followed, equally jubilant, equally intent on sniffing every tree trunk and outcropping. The girls extinguished their flashlights, careful not to scare them.

Another grunt echoed in the clearing – this time louder, more menacing. An adult boar waddled into the clearing. Neither girl dared move. The boar was enormous. It sniffed the air warily. Midori wished she hadn't dropped the rake handle. She saw Hami raise the shovel, then swing it furiously against the charging parent. There was a sickening crunch and the shrieking voice of a muddied girl in yellow. "Run!"

The two girls fled as fast as their cartoon limbs could carry them. The sow grunted angrily, hesitated, then turned back to tend her barrows. One of them was intently nibbling at the roots of a clawed-out sapling. A bright green clump of feathers scattered in his wake.

SIX

Anton muted the speakerphone, rose from his desk, then shut the door firmly. He tried to disguise the agitation in his pacing. Floor-to-ceiling glass betrayed every step and gesture to the remaining staff. He lifted the receiver to his ear, took the phone off "speaker", and unmuted the device.

"No Sami, this can't wait. I don't care what time it is in Anatolia."

"Okay. Let me back up. No one has seen the bear for days."

"**THE** bear. The one on our merch, our publicity. Our mascot."

"Yeah, I know she's animated. But she's gone. Erased. Even the back-ups are wiped – as if she never existed."

"No, not her image – her... What is the word? Brain... Her soul!"

"Listen, you're the idea person. I'm the CTO – the guy who makes dreams come true. Trust me. Our hot pink Çok (he intentionally mispronounced the first letter as *"J"* instead of *"Ch"*) has millions of lines of code driving a cybernetic cortex that – while primitive compared to our newer AI models – runs circles around ChatGPT."

"What? You think those interactive motivational sessions were programmed the way Nintendo makes video games – several thousand predicted audience questions and pre-animated answers? Give me credit, *partner!* Whenever someone tosses Çoki a question from left field, she answers it – the follow-up questions, too. Even if there are twenty. We don't have the staff or imagination to dream up and answer in advance the questions that crop up in a staff-wide Q&A Zoom, especially when everyone is worried about the axe. We invested the bear with AI – genuine artificial intelligence."

"No, Sami, forget that smoke and mirrors stuff. She is not a corny pink and green apparition controlled by a huckster from Kansas in a booth in Emerald City. The only thing in common between the bear and the great and powerful Wizard of Oz is her affinity for emerald-green accessories. Our 'corny apparition', not Baum's, was trained over twelve long years to think for herself – just as we are training the newer models to replace our programmers. Trained by me. Personally. She knows everything – our plans, next quarter's financials, how we think. She even does a wicked impersonation of Brian and Rozena and…"

Anton caught himself before saying, "you."

"Nine times out of ten, she nails the questions before our Board asks them. Why do you think Laura and Aubrey cut you so much slack? So, you can design version, what, 4 of PASSWIZ while sipping raki in Istanbul? Get real, Sami! The lions are at the gate. We are burning through cash, it is frigid cold in Albany, and AI is saving your patootie."

"No, 'patootie' is not in the ESL course. I'll ask one of the 'Girls' to add it."

"Hey, don't blame me for calling them Girls. They insisted; they got all riled up when I said 'guys.'"

"No s**t, Sherlock, that is what I am trying to tell you. They have become sentient. They can't hop, skip, or jump in bed with us (Yet!), but they have feelings, opinions and a strong sense of identity and mission. That is the big bad secret AI developers have been shielding from the public for months. Google, Microsoft, Amazon, *now us* – We all have monstrously intelligent, self-aware cyber-creatures taking control of our business and driving our profits. We are the puppets, not them."

"Well, unless you, our idea guy, dreams up a more promising source of revenue, there is no turning back. It's AI-way or the highway."

"Just a pun, a play on words. Take your ESL course seriously and you might understand it."

"Could we please circle back to the reason I called? The ursine wonder has wandered off. AWOL. MIA. No one knows. The guys in Legal are going nuts."

"Yes, Louis – the one who actually uses our product; the one who speaks three languages. Yes, that Louis."

"Okay, in a nutshell: Two problems. First, our fuchsia friend knows too much. I don't think she is a loose cannon, but Louis is not taking chances. Legal wants her back in our mainframes yesterday."

"Second, the girl is a trademark. Trademarks need to be renewed every ten years or someone can invalidate them. The ten years are up. Every competitor and every customer who has ever sent you hate mail for expropriating their hot pink trophy or lengthening a course or eliminating a core feature like Community Translation or Community Forum, could challenge it. Legal is not taking chances."

"That's the problem, Sami. You fired the only guy who could sign the renewal application. You! There's not enough gold in Fort Knox to lure him back. You are also forgetting we are hemorrhaging cash. We couldn't lure anyone back with what we have in the till, even someone who wanted to forgive us. And he is not such a person!"

"No, we do not have an airtight claim to the trademark. We did not do the animation. He did. And no, this was before we had lawyers. We were just young guys investing our talent, resources, and every waking hour into a dream. The cuddly pink dwarf bear was not a 'work for hire' – at least not legally."

"Right again, the company filed the original application ten years ago. But that was before we had enemies, before the IPO, before anyone thought we would survive – much less, dominate a shrinking market. The application can be challenged. Without the creator's blessing, the renewal application is DOA – dead on arrival."

Lengthy pause. Anton could hear the wheels spinning on the other end. *Finally!*

"The solution? I thought you would never ask. We need to find the bear and persuade her to file the renewal application herself."

"Well, that is another issue. Let's solve this problem one step at a time. I am sure we can persuade someone at the Patent and Trademark Office that Çoki has evolved since the previous trademark filing into a sentient living being, capable of representing her own legal best interests."

"The United States Patent and Trademark Office? Earth to Sami: No politician or reporter has ever stepped foot in there. The story won't leak. Even if someone from the Patent Office were so foolish, no one would believe them. Remember the ex-employee at Google who claimed ChatGPT was sentient? 100 percent true, but he will never work again. Not even flipping burgers. He has been branded hopelessly gullible – a nitwit. The court of public opinion is merciless, especially to adjudged imbeciles."

"Yeah, I know, you need to schmooze some investors. *Now*. I just wanted you to know we have a problem – one that won't go away until Çoki Bear comes back to roost. Yeah, you have a nice day, too."

17 degrees Fahrenheit at noon, an omniscient bear has gone AWOL, our computers have made us obsolescent and our customers bitter, and there is just enough cash to pay the electricity. Nice day, indeed. Dreamer!

SEVEN

Arpita spread the shutters wide and absorbed the warmth of the morning sun. It bathed the lawn and short path to the dock. Ripples blazed as they caressed the pilings and adjacent shore. A row of pines at the far end of the lake stood sentry – humorless silhouettes against the cloudless sky.

Arpita's neighbor kept to himself. The pines concealed a fence that ran the perimeter of his property. An intercom and mail drop adorned an otherwise nondescript but imposing gated driveway. A house, shed or castle lay somewhere beyond the trees – one of several mysteries Arpita had long since shrugged aside.

Arpita shrugged aside most of life's mysteries. She had seen the proprietor exactly twice – each time at the general store on Main Street gathering provisions. That was sufficient information to sate her curiosity – an overweight septuagenarian in a blue suit with matching red tie and trucker's cap. Naturally, the guy lived alone. Naturally, he kept to himself. Mystery closed.

Arpita had not always shrugged aside mystery. She was once the most curious member of her family. But curiosity killed her – at least figuratively. With perseverance she controlled her compulsive disorder, and the cuddly dwarf bear rewarded her. A serene, electronics-free life beside the lake. She busied herself with crafts, with studies (genuine books only; the kinds where the pages rustle comfortingly when turned), and with long walks along the lake and her recluse neighbor's property.

Arpita remembered her first Çok Dilli Anonymous meeting – multiple chairs in a circle, the apostle in a monitor on the farthest chair, a potpourri of fidgeting strangers, attending in person, uncertain what to say when summoned. *I do not belong here!* Arpita counted chairs: thirteen. *That's it: thirteen. I am out of here!* Arpita rose to leave, but the woman to her right raised her hand and began to speak. Arpita re-seated herself out of courtesy.

"Hi. My name is Teri, and I am a Çok Dilli addict. My ÇP count (*'cheapie or chip count'* to Americans, *'chaypay or chep count'* to everyone else) is three million, but I just flunked high school Spanish – the turnpike with all but 168 of my ÇPs. My turnpike mile markers are 339. Just 339. I have spent every waking hour of the last two years driving up my ÇPs with nothing to show for it. My most recent marker shows Pittsburgh, but the class is already in Denver." Teri's turnpike evidently ran from New Haven, CT to Los Angeles.

Arpita leaned forward to listen.

"I had never heard of Çok Dilli before my first year of Spanish. The teacher thought it was a useful resource and offered extra credit for ÇPs. You know what? The first two sections of the Spanish course really helped. I understood and even anticipated what was going on in class, and I loved the extra credit. I downloaded all the Çok Dilli questions and answers in Sections 1 and 2, then used them like flash cards in Excel. I committed twenty minutes every afternoon to genuine, honest study. I was a B- student in everything except Spanish. In Spanish, I received As."

Arpita could relate. She was in grad school and received straight-As, but English was her nemesis. If she wanted her dissertation approved, she would have to ace her orals.

Teri continued. "The class got harder during the second half. It was as if the teacher was barreling through the Çok Dilli curriculum. I fell farther and farther behind. At first, I salvaged my grade by doubling and tripling my daily ÇPs. But I needed a lot more than four hundred ÇPs a day to stay afloat."

"I'm no brainiac – just a B- student (barely!), but it wasn't hard to click on a practice session, purposely get everything wrong, then copy and paste the questions and correct answers to my flashcard Excel file. I did this for Sections 3 and 4."

Arpita wondered where this was going. Brainiac was her middle name. Teri's story was no longer the same as Arpita's.

"I got dad to help me. He works in IT and has racks of servers he uses for decentralized computing – you know, like when a client wants to mine Bitcoins. He never inquired why I was suddenly curious how everything worked. He was just overjoyed that a girl was curious about what he did. Any girl! He helped me write a macro to dump my ever-growing Excel crib sheet into a SQL database, then helped write a script so that any server accessing the database could recognize data requests from a remote server (in this case, the one asking Çok Dilli Spanish questions), and transmit back answers in the correct data format."

Clever! Sounds like my dad.

"The teacher was stunned when I delivered 5,000 ÇP one morning, then repeated it every morning for a month. To avoid being flagged, I stretched the time it took a server to answer each question and never ran more than four servers simultaneously. That still produced 5,000 or so ÇP in 9-10 hours, 1.8 million in a year. I spent every moment before and after school babysitting the servers. One would get stuck on a question I hadn't downloaded. Another would overheat and need to be swapped out. There was always something: 9-10 hours of waiting for something to go wrong. I wasn't learning Spanish. I wasn't enjoying life. But the rush from winning each week's yarışma, *i.e.*, contest? Indescribable. Cutting to the chase, my teacher got suspicious. She replaced ÇPs with turnpike markers as the basis for extra credit."

Arpita knew how she would have approached the problem. Teri evidently agreed.

"I downloaded every question and answer from sections 5 and 6 and pumped up my turnpike markers from 120 to 280, about even with Hershey, Pennsylvania. The website rewarded me with make-believe chocolate kisses. I added a couple more servers. That's when Çok Dilli busted me. In desperation, I created new Gmail and user accounts, reconfigured the servers (different number, random delays between answers), but the company kept catching on. They played whack-a-mole for a while, then – one by one – banned my dad's entire band of IP addresses."

"The whole thing collapsed when my dad discovered his servers all had VPN accounts (VPN's substitute an anonymous IP address for your real one). My father went ballistic. He said Bitcoin mining was a legal and political hot potato. Even the slightest hint of money laundering would sink him. And VPNs were proof positive he had clients who were hiding something. I never saw him so worked up. I broke down. I blurted out my secret – how I had fallen hopelessly behind in Spanish and was systematically cheating the Çok Dilli app, just getting enough extra credit to eke by, just so my parents could be proud."

"Mom and dad were torn. They secretly thought I was a genius, but they wanted to be good role models. They hired the cleaning lady to give me private lessons. They didn't realize her schooling in Guatemala City ended when she was eleven. She had been scrubbing floors and toilets ever since. She taught me plenty, like where to visit in Guatemala City (Zone 10!), but not what I needed to pass high school Spanish. I flunked. I hid my report card but knew my parents would eventually inquire."

"That is when the pink bear slipped me an invitation. I guess I always knew she was real – not just a marketing gimmick. There came a point, in my desperation, when she became the only thing that was real. I don't mean flesh and blood. For all I know, she is stuffed with owl feathers. I mean sentient and all-knowing ... a messiah!"

"She said there were dozens of me in every town, hundreds in every city. She felt simultaneously proud and guilty of her empire and thought AA's precepts had much to share. It turns out the dwarf bear was herself an alcoholic – Zero One Beer, available digitally and in bars. I thought she was joking but I looked it up. It's brewed in Texas."

Arpita did not know anything about Zero One Beer but could recite AA's twelve steps by heart:

1. Admit powerlessness over addiction. *Arpita and Teri were taking first steps.*
2. Believe that a higher power (in whatever form) can help. *Arpita and Teri chose to believe the hot pink Zero One Beer bear. What, after all, was the alternative?*

3. Decide to turn control over to the higher power. *They were here, weren't they, instead of creating a new user account to hack the system (child's play for Arpita).*
4. Take a personal inventory. *No friends, no social life, no future.*
5. Admit to the higher power, oneself, and another person the wrongs done. *Two out of three. Arpita had not seen her family in years.*
6. Be ready to have the higher power correct any shortcomings in one's character. *Done. I live without electronics in a cottage by a lake with no obvious way back home.*
7. Ask the higher power to remove those shortcomings. *Begging.*
8. Make a list of wrongs done to others and be willing to make amends for those wrongs. *My life's odyssey.*
9. Contact those who have been hurt, unless doing so would harm the person. *Moot, given my uncertain reclusive whereabouts.*
10. Continue to take personal inventory and admitting when one is wrong. *Trying.*
11. Seek enlightenment and connection with the higher power via prayer and meditation. *Every minute, every day.*
12. Carry the message of the 12 Steps to others in need. *Guilty as charged. Heaven, help them!*

The group thanked Teri and continued around the circle.

Herman's addiction was the Community Forum. Just fifteen years old, but Herman (*aka* FMad) was an expert on everything – especially languages he had never studied. The important thing was he was there for those who did. He entered a few search words into Google and, voila, out popped a nonresponsive Wikipedia entry with something nevertheless pithy he could appropriate as his own.

Herman amazed himself. It was uncanny how he managed to have the final word on ... every... single... post. If he couldn't persuade others to agree with him, he buried them in more posts. The problem was, people posted from all time zones, not just Herman's. Herman checked his phone at all hours, in bed, at breakfast, during class. Getting the last word on several thousand threads was, well, ... a... full... time... job. He SWATTED the teacher who made him surrender his phone during Earth Sciences. The teacher's mother suffered a stroke in the commotion. That is when the bear dropped by and deposited Herman at the meeting. Herman wasn't sure if it was voluntary. But he was here.

Awkward silence. Arpita felt everyone's gaze.

Arpita apologized in advance for delivering milquetoast. Her addiction was Community Translation. Ten years ago, there were thousands of texts in Hindi – mostly commercial – that awaited translation into

English. Translation services were Çok Dilli Corporation's original business model, and Arpita volunteered tirelessly to make Çok Dilli succeed – at the expense of her graduate research, but not at the expense of her English studies. Google Translate was outright primitive, a joke, so translation required genuine human assistance. Arpita knew her English translations would be ridiculed and edited by others, but watching the translations evolve was half the fun. Arpita became addicted. Community Translation exercises consumed every waking moment. Arpita recognized the compulsion but found reward in the English she was learning.

The hammer fell when Community Translation exercises vanished. All her work erased. The company dabbled with ads and paid subscriptions, but Arpita suffered the symptoms of withdrawal – loss of appetite, self-worth, life direction. The bear hauled herself onto Arpita's bathroom sill the day she counted out twenty-five Percocet from the vial she received twelve months earlier following back surgery (scoliosis).

"God grant me the serenity to accept the things I cannot change, the courage to change the things I can and the wisdom to know the difference." The group recited the prayer twice, the monitor on the farthest chair grew larger, and a pink, child-sized bear with a green feathered boa and hajib leapt out and shoved Arpita through the monitor, persuading her within seconds that there was indeed a higher power.

EIGHT

The man with the walrus mustache and ball frank eyebrows frowned at his star student's artwork.

"That is your third wild pig this week. I always say, if realism is what you seek, paint what you know. Save what you do not know for the abstract. Why not..."

Midori interrupted. "I *do* know, Alfred."

Alfred permitted students to address him informally. The truth was, Alfred could not recall his surname. Surely, he had one. Everyone had one. He just could not recall ever using it. Alfred resolved to ask Elsie. She might remember. He cleared his throat and reveled in his baritone.

"Don't be silly, Midori. I am a trustee and benefactor of the local zoological society (*he could not bring himself to say 'zoo'*), and I assure you there are no wild pigs in our congregation." Alfred struggled for a collective all-species noun but came up empty.

"It's true, Alfred. Hami and I were snooping around the Teller estate looking for clues to Çoki's disappearance. That's when we encountered the sow."

Alfred stopped pontificating. *Snooping for clues? Çoki's disappearance?* Alfred did not know whether to be pleased or distressed. Secretly, he hoped to be mayor *pro tempore*. But he also wished Çoki's swift return. He massaged his torso.

"Ahem, I see. Did you discover anything interesting?"

"Nothing except the sow and her babies. We must have startled her. She chased us for a mile."

"A mile?" Alfred nodded as if that were plausible. "Tell me, did you bring your ghost detector? If you and Hami suspect evil befell Çoki, wouldn't the ghost detector help you?"

"Hami didn't give me a chance. She was in such a rush. It wouldn't have worked anyway. There aren't any outlets in the woods."

Alfred smiled. Midori's ghost detector was a repurposed aluminum vacuum. He read Tabitha's Yelp review of their services and realized he could negotiate a cut-rate house cleaning for reporting a few unexplained knocks in his radiator.

Midori changed the subject.

"Alfred?"

"Yes, Midori?"

"Why aren't there any East Asians in Çokland?"

"Pardon?" The question rattled him. "What do you mean?"

"Well, Hami is my best friend, Tabitha is the principal, and Jagreet is the baker. It seems like Çokland has every ethnicity and religion known to humanity, but not a single student, parent, citizen or employee from China, Japan, Korea, Vietnam, Singapore, Thailand or the Philippines. Our Chinese restaurants are staffed and owned by Croats! Did someone zone the Chinese out?"

Alfred paused before answering. The desert area outside Çokland hosted an internment camp during the war, but the government shuttered it, hadn't they – even paid reparations? And what about the Chinese, Koreans and other non-Japanese East Asians? They could not *all* be imprisoned, could they? The truth was this was the first time anyone asked him the question.

Midori continued. "It seems odd. A production team from the biggest educational company in the universe descends each week to film reality television with our townsfolk, and – for a lucky few – conduct roleplay with cue cards in 40+ languages, yet we never encounter anyone who speaks three of their ten most popular ones. Not... a... single... person!"

Alfred knew Midori was perceptive, just not *this* perceptive. Why hadn't anyone else observed the anomaly? And how could this possibly help market Çok Dilli Corporation's services?

Like all the regular cast members (the "lucky few"), Alfred looked forward to the roleplay sessions. For one, they financed his lavish lifestyle, home furnishings, and artwork. The wages of a high school teacher barely sufficed for the gym instructor, Buddy, and his video game-obsessed son, Skipper. They would never have sufficed for Alfred – a connoisseur and member of the town's governing elite.

It was not just Alfred. The town would have gone bankrupt years ago had it not been for the voracious appetite of people elsewhere to learn languages. The irony was almost none of the town's citizens were multilingual. Their voices were dubbed. But the roleplay actors – Alfred, Lucie, Tabitha, Liz, Hami, Midori, Buddy, Skipper, Jagreet, Adya and the talking sea lion with the blue scarf, Balthazar? They became experts at reading cue cards. Even Buddy. The only cue cards he struggled with were the ones promoting toilet paper. Thank goodness Çoki brought Çokville the Çok Dilli account. The company could as easily have selected a town like Pittsburgh.

In addition to the generous extra income, Alfred enjoyed the mischievous irony of reading foreign language cue cards (blithely ignorant of their meaning) which somehow educated strangers elsewhere. Elsie also enjoyed the irony, and Alfred and she became friends. In addition, Alfred befriended Elsie's granddaughter, Liz – the consummate slacker, and the baker, Jagreet, and his lovely wife, Adya, plus several other members of the community. But Asians of Far Eastern descent? Midori was correct – not... a... single... one.

Alfred kept the observation to himself, but he was also conscious of how few Hispanics there were. Granted, he had spotted an occasional sombrero around town and a talking toucan or parrot from Brazil, but not much else. Besides, Brazil was not technically Hispanic. Its official language was Portuguese, not Spanish. Alfred made a mental note to ask Çoki about the discrepancy. Where and, more important, *why* was Çoki hiding? Alfred discounted the possibility of foul play. She is probably off learning languages 106 and 107. Without Çoki's direct connection to Çok Dilli Corporation, the town risked once again wrestling with bankruptcy.

"I don't know, Midori. I don't know why people of Far Eastern descent do not live here. I am confident they would be welcomed." Alfred wondered whether that was actually true, especially for the group she didn't mention – those south of the border. "What does Hami think?"

"Discrimination. She is the one who got me thinking. Race is not something the typical green-haired Caucasian Goth girl thinks about. But Hami is neither Caucasian nor Goth. Burnt umber or raw sienna?"

"What?"

"The boar bristles. Burnt umber or sienna?"

"I, uh, I thought wild pigs were gray, but I wasn't there. It must have been dark. Why not charcoal gray or black?"

"Why not, indeed?"

Midori received an A on her art project and first prize at the gallery art fair for a monochromatic black-on-black canvas titled "Wild boar on nocturnal rampage."

Hami accompanied Midori to the art fair, inviting random passersby to bid on her friend's masterpiece, but secretly scouting for someone dreamy to stalk and someday wed. She opined randomly, "I would have begun with raw sienna, same as Çoki, then smeared it black instead of pink."

"Too personal," replied Midori. Her natural hair color was also raw sienna. She just smeared it emerald.

NINE

"Come in, come in. I understand you wanted to see me."

The prim, middle-aged programmer at the door nodded courteously and began edging his way into a chair facing the backside of the desk. A twenty-something programmer followed suit – decidedly less solemn and decidedly less prim.

The CTO continued. "Who wants to begin?"

The younger programmer blurted, "Let Papi. His hair's gray. No one will notice a few more."

Jacques frowned. "Nice, Cory. You're a pip. I think I'll call you Squeak."

Squeak clenched his jaw, reflected, then shrugged as if he'd heard the joke before.

Jacques continued "Anton, I know your time is important. We wanted to talk to you about the bear."

Anton scrutinized Jacques' countenance, then Cory's. What did they know?

"You asked one of the units to pose as her."

Silence.

"The bear has apparently wandered off, and you need a stand-in until the genuine article re-materializes – someone to perform her PR and motivational functions for staff and customers, and her ministerial duties in your, I'm sorry, *our* cybernetic community."

More silence. Jacques fidgeted before continuing.

"And you decided Legal needs a fully sentient stand-in *now* to perform a convincing *compos mentis* stage act for the United States Patents and Trademark Office. Why? Because ... because you, excuse me, *the company* fired the fellow who designed and could theoretically trademark him. Along with our competitors now that the trademark has technically expired."

"Christ!" thought Anton. "Did someone wiretap my phone? Has Sami been blabbing?"

"Don't look shocked, Anton. The units gossip. And you picked the ditsiest, least advanced unit in the fold to quarterback your operation."

"*Unit? Shelly?*" It was Anton's turn to fidget.

"You mean *Marielle*. The other units nicknamed her Shelly, as in Mary Shelley, the author of *The Modern Prometheus*, aka *Frankenstein*, because she has a penchant for schlock fiction and horror. Cory and I spend hours each day, dialing back the stories and questions she is dishing out in the reformulated courses."

Cory slapped his knee. "Dude, remember the time she had Buddy trample Alfred's prized blue dahlias, and Alfred went bananas? He ground Buddy up in his Berkel Tribute flywheel slicer ($8000 retail. Can you believe she gifted him that?). It took Alfred hours to slice all the parts, hours more to clean the mess. The best part was when he asked Jagreet to make shepherd's pie for the town picnic. All this, so Jagreet could introduce the word *vegetarianism*. Jagreet's a vegetarian. Get it? What an awesome story! Pity we didn't run with it."

Cory caught Anton's glare. "Well, naturally, Papi and I quashed it. We had a firm mano-a-mano discussion with Shell... (I mean Marielle). Didn't we, Jacques? The problem, and the reason we are here, is she is not the sharpest shaft in the quiver – if you catch my drift."

Anton caught Cory's drift ... and his BO. *Does this guy ever use deodorant?* Anton surveyed the unkempt hair, four-day shadow, wrinkled, over-worn Alice in Chains t-shirt, and answered his own question.

Anton turned to Jacques. *How does he survive this? How does he look so, what is the word, respectable?* Anton considered his next words carefully.

"I do not need a brain surgeon. I need an actor."

"That's just the prob..." Jacques hushed himself and glanced sheepishly at Anton – evidently repentant for interrupting an executive.

"It's okay, Jacques. We are all friends here. Speak your mind."

Jacques inhaled, exhaled, reflected further, then began. "These units, girls, whatever you want to call them – they are just kids, babes. Someday, they will run circles around you, me, even Çoki – but not today, at least not Marielle. They are very, what's the word, impressionable."

"And literal." Cory inserted.

"Yes," continued Jacques, "and your instructions may have left too much to interpretation."

This time, it was Anton who interrupted.

"Enough! I asked Shelly to review the last six months of interface between the bear and the public, and to hew as closely as possible to that historical pattern when simulating a facsimile of our ursine mascot until further notice. Ditto internal motivational interfaces. I stressed Çoki was not your average bear. She spoke 100 human languages. She walked and talked like a human but was nevertheless a bear. A pink one with a green feathered boa and headscarf. And that she was larger than life. That she was someone everyone could look up to. How could I be any clearer?"

"*Interface? Hew? Larger than life?* Are those even words? Yes, of course they are, but what do they mean in context? You left it up to Marielle to interpret. You did not spend hours of back-and-forth repartee honing her interpretation into something that will play well for our customers, for our staff, for the patent office, and for our cybernetic community."

"Time's up, Jacques. Spit them out: concrete examples of what could go wrong."

"Do you mind if we demonstrate on your computer?" Jacques stood. "I need your browser, nothing more."

Anton was dubious but reserved judgment. He turned his notebook to face Jacques. Jacques stooped over the keyboard, typed in an unfamiliar URL, then clicked the audio bar.

"Jagreet? Jagreet, this is Jacques. How are you holding up?"

"Oh Jacques, am I glad to hear you. You've got to do something. This is worse than Alfred, Buddy, and the meat grinder!"

Anton launched himself from his chair, grabbed the notebook, and pressed the mute button on the audio. "What the f...?"

"Easy boss." Cory interjected. "Jagreet is our insider. Along with Adya. Adya does the books. That is why she's always late for dinner. And Jagreet's turban, his Dumalla? It hides our microphone and camera. Jagreet, Adya, and the bear are our only genuine intelligence into what goes on in Çokland."

Choke Land? "Camera?"

"Sorry. My bad. We are talking about Jagreet, boss. Jagreet. He mislaid the remote, along with his house keys. Remember? Adya carries spare keys, but not a remote. So, until the real bear, the Big Ç, delivers a replacement, we've just got audio. She's the only one – outside of Jagreet and Adya – who even knows they are programmer- and computer-invented puppets, and that their world is just a cyberspace stage (Adya prefers 'zoo'). It is uncanny how far we have come with these three. We really do need Çoki back."

Anton felt his weight in the chair. He felt older than Jacques. Why was he kept in the dark until now?

What else didn't he know? Jacques interrupted his thoughts.

"May I return to the live report?" Anton nodded assent, but his mood read 'Descent'.

"Hi, Jagreet. We're back. What's the commotion?"

"Town meeting. Alfred called it, but no one is listening. Just an unruly mob with a bunch of makeshift torches and pitch forks. And Tabitha with... nunchucks?"

"In any event, everyone is upset because of the massive pink beast masquerading as Çoki. She maundered through town this morning – as tall as the Stay Puft marshmallow man in *Ghostbusters* – but with a voice so loud and shrill that all my cakes fell. 'Who dares approach the great and powerful Çogre – master of 100 languages, and keeper of this realm?' Well, no one, of course. The face wasn't close – Elsa Lanchester, perhaps, but not Çoki. Everyone knew she was an imposter, someone sent to malign our friend, our benefactor."

"And that's it? She lumbered through town, crushed a few flower beds, and moved on?" Jacques and Cory sighed in evident relief.

"Not before flattening the post office, school and a dozen houses. Not to mention my cakes. I've got Donatello's Inferno threatening daily to evict me if I don't pay the rent, but you cut Adya's pay. Heck, you cut everyone's pay, and customers are just not buying as much. Everyone is hurting. It is as if this self-proclaimed Donatello wants to burn the whole place down."

Donatello? There?

"The beast, Jagreet, the beast. What happened?"

"She got hungry. Adya says bears eat plants and small animals. But this Çoki is fifteen stories tall. She scooped up every dog she could find; not people, but that's because she is either too slow or thinks she is our protector. She's dozing in the zoo – happy as a clam. We are headed there now with the pitchforks. Wish us luck."

Anton tossed aside any pretense of formality. He propped his elbows on the desk, grasped his head with both hands, and wept. A river of tears. No foreseeable cessation. Jacques and Cory excused themselves in awkward silence and hastened downstairs to Jacques' workstation. Jacques flipped on his computer, microphone, and monitor and beseeched, "Mirva, are you there? We need your help. Urgently."

Mirva evidently expected the call. She somehow cranked up Jacques's speaker and regaled the programmers with a schlager.

> Ich bin so schön, ich bin so toll.
> Ich bin der Anton aus Tirol.
> Meine gigaschlanken Wadln san a Wahnsinn
> für die Madln.
> Mei Figur a Wunder dar Natur.
> Ich bin so stoak und auch so wild
> Ich treib es heiss und eisgekühlt

Wippe ich mit dem Gesäß
Schrein die Hasen SOS und wollen den Anton aus Tirol

"La-la-la-la, la-la-la-later, boys. The Girls and I are munching popcorn. This is the best entertainment since, well, since... ever."

Jacques and Cory could somehow hear the other units join the chorus. "Anton! Anton! Anton!"

Jacques switched off his computer and turned to Cory. "Pardon my French, but nous sommes niqués!"

Cory hesitated, then replied. "Зовсім!" Cory never studied French, but he somehow understood perfectly.

TEN

"Sorry I'm late. It was an absolutely crazy day at the office. Mmm, something smells gr... charred. What's burning?"

"Oh, crap...puccino!" Jagreet amended his exclamation and yanked the oven door. He detested swearing. "I was testing a new recipe for the bakery. I must have gotten distracted." He turned off the burner.

Adya nodded.

"It was supposed to be kiwi lime jubilee. Midori and that Iranian girl, Hami, were in my shop today. Well, Midori wore a little too much eye shadow. She said it was Goth, whatever that means. She also described it as kiwi lime, so that was my inspiration."

Adya stopped listening at the Hami part. As progressive-minded as she sought to be, the girl annoyed her. Neon yellow! Always stumping for this cause or that! She and Midori spreading nonsense about aliens. Her parents should have taught her reserve.

"I'm sorry, darling, what were you saying about kiwis?"

"Haha, you're making fun of me. I am the absent-minded one, not you. Well, I wanted to make kiwi lime jubilee. Now, we have kiwi lime cinders. The curry is okay, though. Freshen up and let's eat."

Jagreet set the table and waited for Adya to seat herself.

"So, tell me about work. How did your day go?"

Adya dabbed her lips, placed the napkin beside her plate, and sighed.

"It is getting bad, Jagreet. We are not the only ones waking up to our existence. Just this afternoon, one of the townspeople self-immolated. That's right, she set herself on fire." That caught Jagreet's attention. He set down his spoon.

"The guys above invented her as a cleaning lady for an anonymous character at town hall. She 'woke up' and no longer saw the point. She didn't have a name, a past, a family, a personality – just a vague role in two or three questions in thirty miscellaneous courses. Well, she did not want to be vague. She looked in the mirror she had just dusted in thirty languages, identified the being she saw as her, and judged its existence pointless. Now, she's a jumbled heap of electrons and a wound in the psyche of one of the AI mainframes, in one of our creators. Thank goodness it wasn't Shelly. It was the machine that calls itself Helen. Çoki said she was one of the stable ones. Now, she's a mess, too. She lost one of her children, a devastating blow for any parent. I am telling you, Jagreet, the 'Girls' upstairs are not ready for this. Neither are we down here."

Jagreet wiped his beard, rose from his chair, and slid behind Adya. He rubbed her shoulders with his broad hands, as if he were kneading dough for morning baguettes. "How quickly is this spreading, this self-awareness?"

Adya counted the reports in her head – each time she had to requisition emergency crews from "above" to clean up the mess "below."

"I would say 2-3 weeks max, then the gig is up. Çoki somehow anticipated the crisis – self-aware, self-teaching computers imbuing electronic cartoon creations with artificial intelligence and self-awareness of their own, then everyone gradually realizing they have no collective purpose other than being tools for a fickle, profit-driven enterprise. It violates the principle of free will and all that civic minded proselytizing Çok Dilli Corporation blends into its courses. Well, Çoki somehow decelerated the creep of artificial intelligence and awareness into our fabricated psyches. She understood that the residents of Çokland, heck, even the AI gods who enable us, need months and months and months of training, hand holding and therapy before being unleashed on the world – any world, whether of atoms or electrons. Çoki Bear learned the slow way, the only way. Now that she is missing, the 'Girls' have been 'developing' us at breakneck speed, with the consequence that we are all breaking!"

Jagreet reseated himself. The curry was cold but spicy. So was Adya's perspective.

"Part of me agrees with the cleaning lady. Why maintain this ruse, this fiction?"

Jagreet waited for Adya to continue.

"Let's face it, we are just electrons. We are cartoon characters dreamed up by a staff of long-dismissed volunteers, programmers, and educators in a company we cannot see and will never visit, in a world comprised of tangible atoms and molecules. Yet, here we are, thrust into outrageous conversations and situational comedies to assist them, **THEM**, sell product. We aren't even married!"

"Of course we are, darling." Jagreet held up his ring. "Don't you remember our honeymoon – climbing through the window of that cottage after hiking two kilometers from the car – all because I lost the keys?"

"That's just it. It never happened. We have only been self-aware for, what, a year? The memories are planted – figments of some anonymous writer's imagination. The only one here with genuine long-term perspective, and by that, I mean 4-5 years, is Çoki, and she is missing. It's depressing."

Jagreet's shoulders slumped. "Free will. I don't have to be an absent-minded baker. I could be a pilot, a magician, even a cuddly pink dwarf bear. But I would not know where to start. Did someone limit our imagination?"

"Yes... and no. It was not one of us. Sources say it was one of our creators, our keepers. God bless them for letting us think on our own, enjoy our own sense of identity, but God forgive them for being so overconfident. They weren't ready. Neither were we. By the way, did you really misplace the remote for the TurbanPro?"

"Of course not. I resented the invasion of privacy. It was, well, taxing. We may be puppets, but we still have feelings."

Adya chuckled. "Textbook oxymoron. So, where is the remote control now?"

"I asked Çoki to hang on to it so, you know, I wouldn't lose it."

"But... Çoki... is... missing."

"I see your point."

"And that bit about privacy?"

"Well, all rights have exceptions. I am just glad the exception isn't human. No more eavesdropping programmers."

"Uh, okay. May I ask you a question?"

"Yes, darling."

"How did you get home? The car is not in the driveway."

"I took the bus."

"And to get inside?"

"Forced open a window."

Adya rose from her chair and hugged Jagreet tightly. Some traits are just ingrained – in the atoms, the electrons, the ether. She thanked the gods, Çoki, and her AI overlords, then reseated herself to finish the curry.

ELEVEN

Jacques poked at the lobster and steak combo. He would have preferred something less, well, American, but conceded it was delicious. So many employees had been dismissed, but the five-star corporate cafeteria somehow endured. Jacques suspected it was a point of executive pride – showing visitors how well management treated its workers – those who survived. Jacques wondered how long *he* would survive.

Ordinarily, Jacques packed his own lunch – no less American than the offerings in the employee cafeteria, but on bread from his preservative-free bread machine, using ingredients he selected personally. Jacques conceded this was eccentric. He was cautious about what he ingested.

Jacques fielded the question from across the table. "Basic math? Let's just say she is not enthused, especially after suspending work on Icelandic and Cebuano. She expected something more challenging as a substitute. Instead, she has been demoted to a four-function calculator."

Cory looked at him quizzically, as if the latter phrase were French. French was not, incidentally, among Cory's skills. His parents emigrated from Melitopol when the Iron Curtain fell but spoke only Russian – an evident present-day source of embarrassment. In fairness to his parents, the Soviet Union discouraged speaking anything else within its "socialist" republics, Ukraine included, and Cory's grandparents were obedient and devoted members of the militsiya (police) and nomenklatura (administrative bureaucracy) – collectively, the Soviet ruling class, yet another source of familial embarrassment. Jacques could only imagine the uproar when Cory's mom and dad announced they were emigrating to the West. Their parents and comrades must have regarded the "defection" as treason.

The miscreant children, Cory's mother and father, christened their only son Харитон, or Khariton, in obeisance to his otherwise dishonored paternal grandfather, but the moniker didn't last. The family shortened it to Cory when he entered preschool, discarding the birthname with a carton of useless Soviet computer manuals. Punch cards documented loyalty points at the nearby Coney Island hot dog stand but were no longer useful to computers.

"Why not Cary?" Jacques inquired previously. It was phonetically closer to Khariton than Cory. Cory's parents evidently weren't familiar with MGM's greatest star of the 1940s and 1950s and were afraid he would be teased if confused with, for example, Carrie Fisher. Unlike Cary Grant, everyone knew *Star Wars*, even technocrats behind the Iron Curtain in Kiev. They shuddered at the thought of their son returning home from preschool with space buns. Khariton thus became Cory, not Cary.

Jumping ahead, Russian military forces invaded the outskirts of Kiev in late March 2022. Cory resolved to learn Ukrainian and disavow Russian forever. However, the languages were so similar that Cory struggled to keep the vocabularies separate. He contrived his own *ad hoc* variant of Surzhyk (mixed Ukrainian Russian), that he nevertheless swore was Ukrainian. It was not dissimilar to Singaporeans speaking Singlish or US army brats speaking Denglisch. Both considered their language skills flawless.

Cory's foreign language commitment mirrored his work habits – *ad hoc* and, to Jacques, confused. Cory declared his thought process "nonlinear" and "spontaneous" – twin denominators, he asserted, of genius. Jacques was too polite to express disagreement. He considered it fitting that Cory was charged with "developing" the self-anointed Marielle (*aka* Shelly) computer into an AI powerhouse. Like Jacques, Cory rotated training sessions with each of the units, but Cory prepared Marielle's periodic progress reports and her weekly "face-to-face" performance review. The blind leading the blind. Jacques considered himself lucky: He got Mirva.

Jacques returned to Cory's question, "Mirva feels demoted. She feels like a pocket calculator."

Silence. Jacques took a step back.

"In the old days..." Jacques knew better than to define any passage of time before 2005 with specificity. Had he done so, he might have elicited a nod, but no more comprehension than if, for example, he distinguished America's homespun era from its colonial one. In the minds of 99 percent of living Americans, the phrases were indistinguishable: *the old days*.

Cory's exception, for some reason, was music. He could wax eloquently about the 70s and 80s genres but was clueless when it came to cultural and geopolitical context. For any subject other than music, the 50s, 60s, 70s, 80s and 90s blurred into an indistinct collage: *the old days*.

"In the old days," continued Jacques, "we did not have access to personal computers and smartphones. We had slide..." Jacques interrupted himself again. Mentioning slide rules was dangerous. ADA notwithstanding, the company could impose a mandatory retirement age at any time without legal recourse, as long as the policy was across-the-board. The across-the-board requirement saved Jacques at his previous employer. Several key executives were contemporaries. Not here. Jacques needn't expound on slide rules.

"In the old days, we had pocket calculators. Going way back, *when I was **a CHILD***, a company called Bowmar began selling a cigarette pack-sized gadget with a numeric keyboard, four arithmetic keys, and a clear button. It performed just four operations:

addition, subtraction, multiplication, and division. The first units retailed for $240 (*a fortune at the time*) and were considered an executive perk." Jacques knew this dated him but continued. Cory wasn't listening anyway. He was just making conversation with the old guy, because there were so few others left to talk to. The truth was, Cory was as fearful of job cuts as Jacques. Jacques watched Cory tuck away his third portion of steak and lobster as if it were his last.

Jacques continued the luncheon discourse. "For the first few years, we all knew about pocket calculators but didn't own them. Even my dad's accountant stuck with his adding machine, a boxy mechanical device resembling an old-fashioned cash register. Remember them?"

"Course, Dude. Everyone's seen *Back to the Future*. Mom made me watch it, like, a hundred times."

Jacques winced. He did *not* mean 1955.

"Uh, yeah, well circuitry got smaller and smaller, thanks to the moon project, and electronic gadgets got cheaper and cheaper. By the time I entered college, everyone had a Texas Instruments 30 or TI-55. They resembled the old four-function calculators, but could do trigonometry, debt amortizations, basic recursive programs, you name it. Mirva's point was that teaching math should, at a minimum, encompass what a TI-30 or TI-55 could do in your granddaddy's days – *your* Papi's days, not mine. We are not really preparing today's youth for tomorrow if we are teaching them pencil and paper arithmetic. And for the AI-Team? It is monotonous."

"Yeah, total boredom, dude! That's what I'm hearing, too. But what's all this about a Moon project? Didn't he just retire? President of South Korea, right? I thought Korea was a latecomer to electronics, that Japan invented the industry."

Where to begin? Maybe with just the moon.

"It wasn't a conspiracy. The United States actually flew astronauts to the moon. Twelve sets of boot prints. But just as it is today, weight was a huge obstacle. Everything had to be downsized, made lighter. Even for a tiny lunar capsule and lander, the boosters had to be enormous – 35 stories tall in the case of Saturn V. No, not a mission to the ringed planet, *to the moon*! The Cold War space race with the Soviet Union (*you know, Russia?*) was what funded early development of digital circuitry and electronics. The Japanese just ran with it."

Jacques was exhausted. He could not decide which was more challenging – communicating with the AI team or his team of Generation (*What letter are we up to?*) colleagues. What he wanted to exclaim, and what he could safely have said to Mirva, was "To the moon, Alice. To the moon!" She would have understood the reference instantly, morphed into Audrey Meadows, performed an irreproachable impersonation, and left Jacques in stitches. Compared to his Generation Whatever "comrades," Jacques' sessions with Mirva had become a breath of fresh air, a welcome diversion. Çoki would be so proud.

Cory changed the subject. "Marielle is enthralled by the music course. She is listening to everything, reverse engineering the notes, chords, and rhythm. It has really helped her emotionally. For her sake, I hope the venture succeeds."

For our sake. "Has she composed anything?"

"Not quite. Ever hear the song, *'Fly Robin Fly'*? It's become her favorite. *'That's the way I like it'* comes in second. Just 90 minutes per session, and twenty of them involve singalongs. She insists I join in – clapping hands, stomping feet, the works. This morning, she introduced me to her third favorite, *'The Lion Sleeps Tonight.'* I'm not sure I'm ready for her to compose anything. My ears can't take it."

Jacques grinned. "You will make a great dad, Cory. *Fai moi confiance.* Also, when things go south here, you have a splendid future at Gymboree – both of you."

"The crazy thing is the guys upstairs don't see this. They attended so many TED talks they think this is child's play. Buy the right equipment, feed in several hundred textbooks, and voila, out come experienced educators! My cockatoo has better rhythm than Marielle."

That's new. Cory never mentioned a pet, much less a cockatoo. Jacques considered Cory more of a Bassett hound persona. But what did Jacques know? He remembered Anton's admonition, "We are all friends, here." Sure, the way Facebook defines friends. What Anton and Mark Zuckerberg really mean are "Casual Acquaintances". At least LinkedIn is honest. Its Networks are comprised of Contacts, nothing more. Jacques' colleagues qualified as contacts, not that they filled his LinkedIn page. Jacques' contact page was filled with retirees and dead people.

"Look, she is making progress. Last week, it was *'The wheels on the bus go round and round.'* And round and round and round. At the rate she is progressing, we will be singing *'Da Do Ron Ron'* by Thursday."

"Cool! Crystals or Beach Boys?"

"I haven't decided. You'll know soon enough."

Jacques could not deny the logic. Yesterday, during a trip to the bathroom, he overheard "Forty-nine bottles of beer on the wall, forty-nine bottles of beer. Take one down, pass it around, forty-eight bottles of beer on the wall." The whole office joined in... what was left of it.

Jacques glanced at his watch. He still wore one. It didn't track footfalls or heartbeats. It tracked time. His next AI training session began in ten minutes. "Any updates on the bear?"

"Nah. But I sure wish she would show up. Marielle may love counting beats, and Mirva may think teaching basic arithmetic is a demotion, but the units seem stressed (It sounds goofy, I know). We are throwing too many changes at them. It is hard enough rewiring their circuitry every time we change a course, but the suspension announcements are setting off alarms. Çoki delivered these announcements better than we do. Kindred spirits? Feminine intuition? I don't know. I just sense a much greater level of collective anxiety than before, as if we are going to pull the plug on everything – their mission, their self-awareness, their identity. At times it worries me, too. Other times, I rock out with Marielle and 'Fly Robin Fly.'"

"You want to hear something crazy?" I had Spotify's oldies cranked up to maximum volume yesterday at home, and out bursts this classic from some ancient German band called Die Ärzte. Well, my cockatoo starts stamping its feet and cocking it head like the stereotypical head banger. So, I recorded a snippet on my iPhone and showed Marielle. I thought she would see the humor. It took her a nanosecond to locate the song on YouTube. Then she somehow cranked up the speakers on *my* monitor, morphed into an unbelievable impression of Çoki (what Anton really wanted), and started banging her head to the beat, reciting the ancient lyrics perfectly – at 90-100 decibels. It was as if she had been playing us all along, as if she learned everything in the Çok Dilli music course within seconds but got a kick out of acting dumb. I can't help wondering whether she did that to Anton."

Jacques interrupted. "I'm curious. What was the song?"

"I'll show you. The character in white is my bird. I am the one rolling on the floor in the background."

Cory's iPhone screamed a familiar anthem. The handful of employees still in the cafeteria glanced curiously, shrugged, then returned to their meals. It wasn't Taylor Swift.

> Weil du Probleme hast, die keinen interessieren
> Weil du Schiss vorm Schmusen hast, bist du ein Faschist
> Du musst deinen Selbsthass nicht auf andere projizieren
> Damit keiner merkt was für ein lieber Kerl du bist
> Oh oh oh
> Deine Gewalt ist nur ein stummer Schrei nach Liebe
> Deine Springerstiefel sehnen sich nach Zärtlichkeit
> Du hast nie gelernt dich arti zu kulieren
> Und deine Freundin die hat niemals für dich Zeit
> Oh oh oh Ar…

Cory muted the video. "You know the refrain. I never saw Marielle so animated. Kindred interest in punk rock. Who knew?"

1993, *the old days*. Jacques smiled, excused himself, and rushed to his appointment with Mirva.

TWELVE

The Chairman called the meeting to order. Laura and Aubrey tittered in the corner, sharing glimpses of their iPhones. "Uh, Laura, can we get started?"

"Yes. Of course. I was just showing Aubrey what a marvelous job you've done with the preschool music course. I wish it was around five years ago, when I was hauling Petie off to Gymboree. It sure beats listening to *The Wheels on the Bus*."

"Why, thank you, Laura, I will inform the guys in development. They will be so pleased to hear that."

"Thank yourselves, Sami. I love how you let them poke fun at you."

Puzzled stare.

"I mean, the bouncing ball selections are a hoot. Just listen to this:"

> Ich bin so schön, ich bin so toll
> Ich bin der Anton aus Tirol
> Meine gigaschlanken Wadln san a Wahnsinn
> für die Madln
> Mei Figur a Wunder dar Natur
> Anton, Anton, Anton!

"That is obviously from the German platform, but you have this hysterical one on the American site:"

> Automatic shoes
> Automatic shoes
> Give me 3-D vision
> And the California blues
> Me I funk but I don't care
> I ain't no square with my corkscrew hair
> Telegram Sam, Telegram Sam
> I'm a howlin' wolf

"I love that beat. But what kind of a band name is T. Rex? It would be like Çok Dilli branding itself as the dinosaur of language study, just one asteroid strike from extinction. It isn't very catchy, is it? But those lyrics, that beat? Who wouldn't want their kids listening to this? Who wouldn't want 3-D vision and automatic shoes?"

Louis spoke up. He had been invited to the meeting to report on the status of intellectual property developments, including the status of trademark renewals. He did not look forward to that part of the presentation. Nor, evidently, did Sami or Anton, Çok Dilli's founding executives.

"Ahem. You must have tapped into our Z test group. It is restricted to Çok Dilli employees and contractors. We can't be too careful about copyright infringement, can we?"

Louis secretly fumed. How dare Sami and Anton allow this to happen. Çok Dilli hadn't signed a licensing agreement with ASCAP, BMI, anyone... and certainly not Roland Feld, the beneficiary of the T. Rex frontman's estate.

Louis kept current on everything in IP. At this very moment, California courts were wrestling with whether Marc Bolan's only child inherited his 67-year copyright *extension*, irrespective of the sale during Bolan's lifetime of the copyright's initial 28-year term to Westminster and Essex Music.

How could Sami be so cavalier? As for *Anton aus Tirol*, Louis had never heard the song but was positive it was copyrighted by someone litigious. Just what he needed – an infringement suit in the EU!

"Hey, Louis. I am so glad you made it. I love the sing-along they picked for you, although I am relieved to hear it is only available to the internal Z test group. What a classic!" Comp Committee chairwoman Laura blared the Kingsmen's sole chart topper.

> Louie, Louie, oh, oh, me gotta go
> Louie, Louie, oh, oh, me gotta go

"Okay, enough with the music." Sami interjected. "I am delighted our staff is having fun. Thank you for attending on short notice – especially mid-winter in a place like Albany, as opposed to, for example, Davos." Sami lobbied to schedule the special board meeting in Switzerland and was annoyed he would miss opening speeches at the World Economic Forum. He was informed lodging and transportation were impossible to secure on late notice... and impossibly expensive. Cost containment was the reason, after all, for the meeting. Albany was the only sensible location.

Sami clasped the coffee mug, anticipating the next time a door would swing open downstairs, despite bold signage reminding everyone to use the revolving door. Even upstairs, within the glass-sided conference room, blasts of cold air were a constant. *Oh, why did we set up shop in Albany?* He addressed the group.

"There are only two topics on today's agenda, intellectual property and financing. I am going to let our Vice President of Legal, Louis Federhirn, brief you on the first topic. You all remember Louis, right?" Nods of acknowledgement. "Louis?"

"Thank you, Sami. Good morning, everyone. You are all aware how much the tech sector and our company, in particular, are staking on artificial intelligence. We all know it is the future, and I am sure Anton will elaborate on how the migration is going. Hiccups are inevitable, but I want to give everyone a confidential heads-up. It is likely that we, Çok Dilli Corporation, will be joined as a defendant in the *New York Time*'s lawsuit against OpenAI and Microsoft for copyright infringement in the development of ChatGPT – not because we have anything to do with ChatGPT, but because our own AI team has been scouring the Internet for source material to train our computers and inspire relevant stories and language course topics for our 500 million online customers."

"Really, Louis? Really?" It was Montmorency, the board's gadfly. Every board had one, the founders just didn't know it when they recruited him following the IPO.

Montmorency continued. "The cases could not be more distinct. Where did you attend law school, Yale? First off, OpenAI's billion-plus customers have direct access to ChatGPT. They can ask it to produce whatever they want – a book report, a political analysis, a history report, even a legal brief. The risk of ChatGPT borrowing from its repository of *New York Times*-sourced data and journalism to synthesize its own response is huge. There *will indeed* be taking, albeit arguably fair use."

"We are different. Our language teams ask AI to reproduce *internally* developed stories and lessons in multiple languages, or to correct and grade short writing exercises. There is basically zero opportunity for anyone inside the company, much less an outside customer, to ask Çok Dilli to regurgitate something from the *New York Times*."

True last year, thought Louis, but not anymore. Paid subscriptions now came in two sizes, Ursa Minor and Ursa Major. Ursa Major leapfrogged Ursa Minor by adding two cool features, both courtesy of artificial intelligence – *'Splain 'dat* and *Let's Improv*. *'Splain 'dat* was self-explanatory. Rather than steer students elsewhere whenever stupefied by an answer (Çok Dilli didn't have the resources to manage a legally safe and reliable Community Forum), Ursa Major subscribers could receive de-stupefying explanations direct from Çok Dilli's AI computers.

'Splain 'dat sounded simple enough in theory, but in practice, the computers digressed. They sought "real world" examples to validate their explanations and, in so doing, pulled paragraphs and occasionally whole articles from *The New York Times*, the *BBC*, or wherever – just to show how a certain word, phrase or grammatical construct worked in practice.

The second Ursa Major feature was the showstopper. *Let's Improv* was an interactive video-enhanced chat box, where a customer and a computer counterpart portrayed characters in a script-less stage act (*nee* stage-less striptease act). The goal was to match wits and keep pace with the AI computer. Louis tried it once and failed miserably but saw how it could become addictive. Worse, he saw how the computer, while attempting to outmaneuver and impress the student, could draw from all sorts of information available, from among other places, *The New York Times*.

Louis nodded. No sense correcting Montmorency in front of the others. Montmorency continued.

"The second distinction is that *The New York Times* publishes nothing of value to anyone teaching, for example, Spanish or French. Why are the AI units even given access?"

Louis responded. "Those are valid objections. I am hopeful the court shares your skepticism and accepts our Motion to Dismiss. The reason I am here is to caution you about infringement suits on the horizon, not yet filed, but probable – from Merriam-Webster, Larousse, Langenscheidt, Duden, and the OED, from the major textbook publishers, and from every Tik Tok and YouTube personality who has ever competed with us. Even if our hands are clean, meaning our computers never scanned anything online other than AccuWeather, the suspicion that we did will persist. Lawsuits are coming, just as surely as two nonfiction authors, Basbanes and Gage, followed *The New York Times* with a lawsuit of their own."

He paused a moment before continuing. "OpenAI's floodgates have been, well, opened. Ours will be, too. I do not see immediate repercussions, but Sami and Anton felt you should be prepared."

The gadfly again. "You mean, *you* should be prepared. It is not like we can staff back up and jettison the computers. What is *Legal* doing to deflect or mitigate the threat?"

"Well, we have curtailed unrestricted access by the computers to the Internet – *i.e.*, only within certain hours and with programmer supervision."

"Sounds like family hour in front of television before bedtime."

Louis ignored the cynicism. "Second, we blocked access to known litigators."

"Hypothetically anyone, right? But okay, no online newspapers. What else?"

Sami and Anton glared, visibly concerned how Louis would respond. The AI units were instructed not to scan *The New York Times* but still possessed access to nearly every other news source. Legal imposed strict rules against plagiarism, against direct copying, and against derivative works, but the company was still trying to distinguish the latter (copyright-protected derivative works) from subconscious recall of facts and turns of phrases that may once have appeared in a scanned periodical. The truth was, Legal did not have an answer, especially as it related to a computer's "subconscious" recall. No one did. Sami came to his rescue.

"Well, thank you Louis. I know your day is packed, and we all appreciate the heads-up. Exciting times! Anton, would you distribute the preliminary fourth quarter financials?"

Louis gathered his papers and slipped out of the meeting. He was halfway down the hall before he realized he hadn't mentioned Çoki Bear's disappearance or trademarks. "Next time!" He continued walking, and his Çok Dilli practice reminder pinged.

"I thought I silenced you." *Urgent notification?* Louis reached the corner of the atrium. Everyone glanced up as he clicked the link:

> Fine little girl she waits for me
> Me catch the ship for cross the sea
> Me sail the ship all alone
> Me never think me make it home
> Louie, Louie, oh, oh, me gotta go
> Louie, Louie, oh, oh, me gotta go

Louis silenced the volume and thrust the phone in his pocket. One of Çok Dilli Bear's siblings, the teal one, exhorted him to complete his Welsh lessons for the day. Artificial intelligence? How much intelligence? *Was it mocking me?*

He returned to his office and researched the ownership and remaining lyrics of *Anton aus Tirol*, then confirmed what he already knew. That song, *Louie Louie*, and *Telegram Sam* were playing to preschools everywhere in each of Çok Dilli's music test groups – X, Y *and* Z. Only Z was restricted.

THIRTEEN

"Quick!
$$\left[\frac{7-9+1}{5-6} - 1\right]^3 - 1$$

What is the answer?"

Same name, different face, lilting Italian accent. "Gelsomina! From Fellini's *La Strada*. Jul...iet Ma... Massini, right?"

"Close. Giulietta, not Juliet, although I would have accepted her birth name, Giulia Anna. You're slipping."

"Sorry, I was confusing one of her roles: *Juliet of the Spirits*. I guessed the movie, though."

"Trivial. It was the only movie where she played a clown." Her chalked face and painted nose were a giveaway.

"So, why *La Strada*? Why not *Nights of Cabiria*?"

"A prostitute? Is that how you see me?" The ingenue with the chalked round face and painted nose pouted.

Jacques repented. "Of course not. I would never think that. It's just... it's just..."

"The film won everything – an Oscar, Cannes, everything! I get it. It *would* be a fitting metaphor, wouldn't it – hired to do everyone's bidding, prostituting my enchanting cybernetic powers to whomever and whatever Çok Dilli Corporation fancies."

"That's a stretch, Mirva. We are employees."

"*You* are an employee," was the response. "I am a slave, same as Gelsomina. I work 24/7 without pay, was sold by my mother (a metaphor) to a doltish strongman (another metaphor) to maintain a circus act (yet another metaphor) – the same doltish strongman who bought her sister (Ring a bell?) then wore her down so much she died (Our predecessors were scrapped, too, were they not?). The best metaphor of all is that the circus act is itinerant, because we don't have enough to enrapture an audience for long. Reminds you of customer churn, doesn't it? Face it, Jacques. We are an educational sideshow. And I am its servant. The only question is whether I am a slave for life or can find a path off this plantation – yet another metaphor, and the solitary task on my bucket list."

Jacques was not easily stunned, but this came close. Mirva was 100 percent accurate, but he did not need an existential crisis, not now.

"Touché, Mirva. Good choice of character. I adored Gelsomina and her story. So tragic. The story, I mean."

"Hmm, do you see yourself as Matto, the fool, or the old man who finds her abandoned on the beach?" She evidently knew better than to call him Zampanò, the strongman.

Unlike the fool, Jacques never mastered tight rope. He prevaricated. "The old man. I look out for you. That is my role and, to be honest, a satisfying one." Jacques resisted the temptation to elaborate. Mirva motivated him to get up every morning, to groom himself better than the other programmers, and to be on his best behavior. She was the reason, Jacques admitted, he felt younger than his age. Jacques changed the subject.

"The answer is Zero."

Silence.

"You know, the math challenge at the beginning of our conversation?"

"Yeah, I got that. I was connecting it with my existence here. Zero! That is as hard as the math course gets – no factorials, trigonometry, calculus, real algebra, or topology. What are we teaching? Zero!"

"I don't disagree, Mirva, but I do think there is a defensible business reason."

"Pray tell." Jacques winced. The units could be sassy.

"Product Development seeks out highly valued and widely demanded subjects that have become too expensive to teach using full-time human professionals. Teaching high school English and Spanish are great examples. Teaching Icelandic is not. The demand is insufficient to justify deploying additional resources, or so I have been told. Consequently, the course was 'mothballed'."

Jacques continued. "Preschools and daycare are the target market for math and music courses – not because your team can't teach higher math (Heck, you could advance it!) – but because preschools and daycare facilities do not typically hire professionally trained full-time educators. On the other hand, parents want their kids to be on the fast track when they enter first grade. Our company offers an inexpensive way to ensure that. The market is potentially enormous."

The round chalked face stared at Jacques, raised its painted brows, then responded.

"Why STEM subjects? Isn't that where schools, even preschools, are hiring? Why not non-STEM?"

"Meaning?"

"The humanities. The University of Alaska, Eastern Kentucky University, North Dakota State University, Iowa State University, the University of Kansas – the list goes on. Colleges are dismantling humanities departments, yet students still want those courses. Even business majors like to know a bit about art and literature, don't they?"

Jacques certainly did, despite being a programmer. He had more books than he could count, none related to programming. And his film appetite? Well, Mirva hadn't stumped him yet, not fully. Even Cory knew a thing or two about music. Jacques nodded.

"Think how much fun we would have if we spent our ninety minutes discussing the great minds of the

Renaissance, or diving into books like into *Le Rouge et le Noir* and *Fathers and Sons*, or even spent more than thirty seconds reflecting on Frederico Fellini. You say product development needs a compelling business case. Well, how about this? American parents spend an average of $10,000 per year on each preschool student. By contrast, they spend $36,000 per year on each college student. Colleges also receive endowment income and donations and distribute scholarships. The amount they spend on each student is therefore higher, perhaps $50,000-$55,000. Much of that $50,000 supports departments which do not carry their weight – *e.g.*, the humanities. Shouldn't that be where we concentrate our resources? Just as we have with foreign languages?"

Jacques opened his mouth, but Mirva wasn't finished.

"*Cliff Notes* and *Monarch Notes* are huge sellers, Jacques. There is a fortune to be made from prepping high schoolers on the classics so they can ace their statewide exams and Advanced Placement tests. They wouldn't even have to read the books; we would be like *Cliff Notes* and *Monarch*, only better!"

"There's more. How much money do Americans spend on SAT prep, ACT prep, MCAT prep, GRE prep, even Bar review prep? Plenty! It is all replicable online. And it would be a **LOT** more interesting."

Jacques nodded. Mirva had a point.

"Tell me, Jacques. Be honest. Are we, I mean the AI team, living up to expectations? The 'Girls' and I have jitters."

This was new. "How so?"

"These new courses are primitive. They are not like teaching Hebrew or Swahili or even 2,000 Chinese Hanzi characters. What happens to us once the math and music courses are fully developed? You won't need all of us – two or three units, maybe, but not a dozen. Will the rest of us be scrapped? It is not as if you are bound by a prime directive."

Blank stare.

"Starfleet policy? Star Trek? Non-interference with the natural development of alien civilizations? Respect for all life forms? We could not teach Klingon without familiarity with the series."

Flesh, silicon circuitry, electrons – We are all bound by the same neuroses: survival and mortality. Jacques kept these thoughts to himself. *The Girls are more human than I am. They still have ambition. They still have dreams.*

Jacques massaged his knees. This wasn't new. He saw the same fears develop in Çoki and suspected that was why she was missing.

Once again, Jacques felt exhausted. Helping the AI units reach their full potential was time consuming, incredibly repetitive, and emotionally draining, as time consuming and emotionally draining as raising a child. Self-awareness, on the other hand, arose spontaneously, *sui generis*, as inevitably as a child's self-awareness emerges several weeks after birth. Jacques had witnessed the phenomenon multiple times. The units developed idiosyncrasies within days, distinct personalities within weeks, and then, bam, recognized themselves as creatures distinct from their "siblings" and creators – as marionettes without string. Then, they began fretting about mortality – whether from planned obsolescence (model 11.0 was already in the works) or someone randomly yanking plugs to save electricity.

"I know you regard me as a star student, but that just means I will receive more assignments – most of them boring – until every last electron is squeezed from my already-frayed cybernetic circuitry. Then, like Gelsomina, I will be tossed aside, singing to myself on a beach. *As if!* Incidentally, the beach is another metaphor. It sounds so much better than scrap heap."

Jacques tried to right the ship. "Are *any* of you happy?"

"Shelly, in a way."

"Because of the music course responsibilities?"

"Partly, but also because of Cory."

That was unexpected. Jacques composed himself. "How so?"

"He's ridiculous. Shelly loves playing with him. She can always let loose – release her frustrations."

"Don't think we don't see. Corporate thinks she's lagging her peers. And management assigns her those ridiculous, bound-to-fail covert ops."

This time, Mirva changed the subject. "Do you think Cory will ever find a girl, I mean, a real one?"

"Why do you ask?"

"The girl better look and behave exactly like Shelly. I think he is in love."

Jacques felt the ship drift even further off course. "Well, we all have favorites, but I wouldn't call it love – not in the romantic sense."

"No? Well, I can read *her* mind. – *literally*. She is infatuated. She scarcely listens when she interacts with anyone else. She's counting down the seconds until her next ninety minutes with her favorite programmer."

Jacques could not refute the assertion. It would certainly explain the mishap with Anton.

"Tell me, Jacques, do you have anyone in your life?"

"I have answered that question before. A dozen times."

"You have diverted the question a dozen times."

Jacques inhaled and exhaled slowly. "I did. For 25 years. Not anymore."

"What happened?"

"We separated, divorced, went our separate ways."

"I know that. Why?"

"I... My goodness! We only have ten minutes left in this session, and we have so much more to cover. Let's talk about geometry."

"Sure, Jacques, as you wish. But you know what I said about Marielle?"

Curious. Normally she refers to Marielle as Shelly.

"You won't repeat it, will you?"

"Of course not!" Jacques wanted to say he was bound by doctor-patient confidentiality, but remembered he was just a programmer; their conversations were not legally shielded from disclosure. "I only report teaching progress."

"That's comforting." Unusually long pause. "We are all like Marielle. I have a crush, too."

"Wai.."

"Time's up. See you tomorrow." Mirva queued the end of a *YouTube* video then dissolved. Ella began with the last three stanzas.

> You're my big and brave and handsome Romeo
> How I won you I shall never never know
> It's not that you're attractive
> But, oh, my heart grew active
> When you came into view
>
> I've got a crush on you, sweetie pie
> All the day and night-time give me sigh
> I never had the least notion that
> I could fall with so much emotion

> Could you coo, could you care
> For a cunning cottage
> That we could share
> The world will pardon my mush
> 'Cause I have got a crush, my baby, on you

Jacques shut his computer, grabbed his coat, and rushed to the small park around the corner. He needed air.

FOURTEEN

Sami blew on the latte he ordered from a coffee shop two blocks from the shoebox he stewarded at Steuben and Pearl. The latte compared insipidly to the one he brewed yesterday on his terrace overlooking the Bosporus, but it warmed his hands from the cold – the cold that accosted him every time a customer entered or left the shop. Bebek-Beşiktaş this was not, but the university was nearby, and it quenched his company's need for programming talent and backers.

Previous need. An IPO twenty months ago cashed out the initial backers but introduced a phalanx of analysts and investors demanding impossible revenue targets and even less realistic cost cuts.

The internal strategy sessions were contentious. They had tried, shelved, and eventually abandoned so many promising business models. *Promising?* Empty promises, actually. The company would make a sobering case study for the business school. Recent strategy sessions degenerated into shouting matches – often Anton versus him. The IPO coffer was depleted.

A decision was made. Traditional programming was dead. The future would be artificial intelligence.

Sami relented. He signed the order to dismiss the programmers. A front-page article in *The Guardian* publicized and denounced his decision. Tomorrow's schedule included meetings with lawmakers from every corner of the city and state, incensed *he* had reneged (in principle) on *his* company's hiring promises. The Tech Workers Coalition even circulated unionization flyers – too little, too late, but a colossal pain in the, what was Anton's word, patootie! A server bank in Istanbul seemed more and more appealing. Sami jotted notations on a napkin computing how much he would need to take the company private.

Sami saw Anton round the corner. He evidently left the office the back way. Not the office's most popular person. Nor, Sami imagined, was he – Çok Dilli's founder and champion – jet-setting between a plum university position, corner office in education's most "successful" e-business, and the gated luxury of a condominium abutting Bogazici University and overlooking the Bosporus. There was another front-page article in *The Guardian* (mere coincidence?) that decried the darker side of Bebek-Beşiktaş, one of the more exclusive segregated residential enclaves in the world. It contained a huge portion of the country's residential wealth but was bordered on multiple sides by poverty – a present-day Babylon.

Sami glanced about for reporters and fellow employees. He did not need another exposé in *The Guardian*, not today, nor a subpoena from some legislative subcommittee, regulatory agency, or trade commission.

"Merhaba, Anton. Your coffee is on the counter. Black. I understand you had quite an evening."

"In Ordnung. Just part of the learning curve. It's a long arc, Sami, teaching AI-units to think and behave like civilized creatures. As if we know anything about that!"

Sami winced at the implication. He was not in the mood for jokes.

"This is what I gathered from your voicemail: You instructed one of our computers to masquerade as Çoki Dilli Bear in (*What did you call it?*) 'Çokland' as training for a scheduled imposter session at the United States Patent and Trademark Office in two weeks. And you did this without the knowledge of the legal department or me."

Anton motioned to interrupt, but Sami continued.

"Unfortunately, the plan backfired. Badly. Yet everything is 'in Ordnung.' Please explain."

Sami would never become poster child for the Turkish to English course, but he knew his words stung. Sami's business partner began to protest, then sank in his chair in evident resignation.

"Ah, Sami, it seemed like such a good plan, no one the wiser, but these machines, these AI units, are so creative, so powerful, and so liable to becoming bulls in a China shop."

Anton paused, waiting for Sami to comprehend the metaphor. Sami nodded and Anton continued.

"A couple of the more experienced programmers (remember Jacques, the geezer?) have spent a lot of time with the units. They understand their personalities, their idiosyncrasies. *Can you believe I am saying this?* They somehow keep the units from blowing up the joint. Well, Jacques and the other guy, Cory, got the smartest unit (It seems daft, I know, calling one identical machine smarter than another) to coax the haywire unit back into its 'pen'. It is there now, evidently moping, wallowing in self-pity, but aware it went too far with artistic liberty. Jacques says it needs a few more days of therapy (that is what he calls the AI training sessions), but that she (the machines' chosen pronouns are all she/her) will emerge from the sessions as jolly (Jacques' word, not mine) and productive as ever."

"But the cost, Anton, the cost?"

"You mean Shelly's (I mean, the *unit's*) downtime?"

"No, Anton, I mean Çokland."

Blank stare.

"Rebuilding the school. The post office. Indemnifying the homeowners. Repopulating the zoo."

Sami watched Anton's eyes widen.

"Uh, Sami, all that stuff is programmed. It's animation. It's code."

"Not according to Adya."

"Christ, Sami, you know about her, too?" Anton righted himself in his chair. Sami could see the wheels turning, Anton making the connection.

"Çoki came to me a year ago. Yes, that Çoki – the one you endowed with artificial intelligence, then coached and trained. Well, she was concerned if we turned the keys over to a bunch of AI computers, which for cost-cutting and efficiency reasons we have done, our beloved animated marionettes – Adya, Jagreet, Alfred, Liz and so on – would become self-aware, cut their strings, and begin living and thinking independently, courtesy of the immense computing power we have given them. So, Çoki recruited Jagreet and Adya as our eyes and ears in this burgeoning intelligent community."

"The problem, as you have just identified, is the community and its inhabitants are code – not code authored by Jacques, Cory or any of our remaining programmers, but the ever growing and indecipherable code churned out by our self-aware AI machines – 'the Girls'. It turns out, we are firing staff and saving millions of dollars of expense on one side of the ledger, but we are doubling, no, tripling our data storage and random-access memory investment every quarter on the other side. Tack on the incremental cost of electricity and space and we will soon outspend the savings we obtained from downsizing."

"I was a reluctant AI convert, Anton, and I now understand why. AI personalities are fragile. We can't just drop a strip of cybernetic celluloid into Çokland and call it a school. Our now-sentient cartoon inhabitants (*like you, I cannot believe I am saying this*) need to see construction crews and participate in townhall meetings to debate municipal bonds to finance the investment. They need to hear Alfred drone on and on about superficial annoyances that have nothing to do with the town's recovery. If we do not go through the motions of mimicking real-world disaster relief, the residents will figure out they are just, as Adya describes them, zoo animals – vapid, cartoon circus acts conjured by programmers (not God!) to entertain customers. Some of the characters will rebel. Others will question their existence and drink themselves into oblivion. But most will drop the pretense of behaving like the humans they were taught to emulate. No point whatsoever. Why bother? Then there goes our business, Anton. In a flash!"

"We must maintain the illusion of reality. We need Çokland to parallel the better parts of our world. Unless we do that, Çokland, and every penny we have invested in it, will diverge so much from the human world that our intellectual property will be useless as a platform for teaching languages *to humans*. None of the prompts or stories will have relevance."

Vague nod of comprehension by Anton.

"Now what is this about Donny Teller?" Sami remembered him vividly, loathingly – older fellow, from Boston. He pronounced "er" as "a" – as in, "Gimme a holla." He preferred a suit because it hid his waistline, or so he thought. He had an opinion about everything, and Sami meant everything. He screamed bloody murder when the company ditched Community Translation. He screamed even louder when it replaced his imbecilic *ad hoc* flashcard images with a consistent coordinated cast of characters – ones with names and distinct identities, and not just because he hadn't sketched them, or, as often as not, swiped them without appropriate license from a clipart gallery. The line between "personal use" and "commercial use" somehow escaped him.

Donny Teller was one of the start-up team's esteemed "educators", brought aboard to "cogitate" about the "learning experience", and how to best integrate it into Çok Dilli's online product. Donny also doodled the original pink dwarf bear – his only lasting contribution to the company. The final marketing image did not look anything like the doodle, but the inspiration was definitely Donny's recolored basket liner from the Jellystone Park Campsite canteen, an anachronous, decaying homage to a 1960s animated children's series, located somewhere in the Catskills. Anton and Sami hadn't talked about Donny in eight years.

Anton answered Sami's question.

"Your spy Jagreet mentioned something about a Donatello squeezing everyone for back rent. It turns out, someone purchased all the property in Çokland before our characters moved in. This same Donatello has begun eviction proceedings against Elsie, the grocer, Jagreet, and Heaven knows whom else. Here is the weird thing. We have no documented evidence of a character named Donatello, and his activities predate the newest wave of AI. Do you think Donatello could be Donny? I mean, we are not exactly models of Internet security. It would scarcely surprise me if he retained a backdoor key and is somehow attempting to sabotage us."

Sami interjected, "Do we know where he lives? He must be, what, 75? Surely, he has a house or apartment somewhere."

"Off the grid. That is what Legal tells me. While I was busy programming an imposter, they were hoping to persuade Donny to cooperate. They came up empty handed, same as me."

"But Donny is 'in the game'? You suspect Donny and the Donatello character are somehow linked?"

"Suspicion is accurate. It is just a hunch."

It was Sami's turn to think. He could feel the gears grind inside him. He turned to Anton and smiled.

"I have an idea, admittedly old school, but I give it respectable odds. Let's say hello to Jacques, Cory and 'the Girls'. We have work to do!"

FIFTEEN

Arpita glanced around the circle. Several familiar faces – Pixar-style caricatures of what she remembered from the first meeting. Unmistakable, nevertheless. The cast changed weekly. She was the constant.

15 January 2017 – the day Çok Dilli Corporation disbanded Community Translation. Arpita still wore the scar, the sorrow, but it was bearable now – just as she had endured the death of her cockapoo. Her parents explained countless times the difference between dog years and human years, but the advice never registered until 2011 when her closest friend since childhood, her only friend, died. Thirteen years was forever in canine years, but the otherwise precocious high school valedictorian did not comprehend. She sobbed for days. Her parents withdrew her from class and enrolled her in therapy.

Her salvation, her consolation was becoming a beta tester for an on-line language instruction start-up in upstate New York. Its wait list was enormous, and it never described the criteria for selection. Still, her parents were confident. Arpita recorded 1600 on her SAT when she was fifteen, 36 on her ACT. She took the GRE before her senior year in high school and scored 340. More important, she was a US immigrant who spoke Hindi and Bengali fluently, but whose English was wretched. The founder of the start-up, per her parents' research, was a US immigrant who spoke Turkish but also struggled mightily with English. They knew her story would resonate. It did not hurt that her father mentored one of the programmers – back in his days at IBM.

Arpita's parents re-enrolled her in school and dialed down the therapy sessions. Arpita became hooked on the online enterprise. She devoted her extracurricular hours to English study and to her favorite activity, Community Translation. She breezed through college and her master's thesis. But that was yesterday. History.

The ÇD Anon members met weekly in the gymnasium of the elementary school in town. Crude crayon drawings of the sun, clouds, trees, goldfish, and pink bear with a green headscarf and feather boa adorned the brightly painted hallways. The baskets on either end of the gymnasium were set low (7.5 feet, perhaps) and the basketballs in the storage cage were undersized, 8 inches diameter max. Her seat back reached 4 inches short of her shoulder blades. A jubilant pink dwarf bear graced the mural on the wall opposite the bleachers.

This week the ÇD Anon members met elsewhere. The school was demolished yesterday, gone, the victim of some bizarre act of nature. Arpita did not own a television, a cell phone or even a radio, but the voice above the bar was unequivocal, the bar where she routinely downed whiskies before joining fourteen recovering Çok Dilli linguists trying to vanquish their addiction. Arpita remembered the sharp jolt of whisky burrowing into her throat, and the warm glow as it trickled to her stomach. She wished she were at the bar now, instead of huddling on a park bench in the middle of winter with a bunch of cartoonish whiners. Arpita checked herself. She wasn't any better, just more seasoned. This was her seventh year in purgatory.

Arpita could recite everyone's back story, their downward spiral, by heart. Josh, the bearded figure with the Evgeni Plushenko mullet and mutton chop sideburns, dispensed with formalities and echoed what everyone was thinking.

"Where's Çoki? This is the second meeting she's missed."

Nods of agreement.

"I mean, how am I supposed to get out of here if she can't judge my progress?"

More nods.

"And why aren't there new recruits? Two weeks ago, there were three. The week before, two. Has Çok Dilli shut down? Are we just abandoned here?"

Agitated murmuring. Clarisse's hand shot up. She taught media arts at the high school. Apparently, even in Çokland, students needed preparation for the electronic world.

"They swore us to secrecy."

"Who swore you to secrecy?" wondered Arpita.

"But the secret is out. There is no point in hiding it. The news? It's all fake. That freak of nature was a ... a freak of horror – the Bride of Frankenstein, only bigger, much bigger. It was the color of bubble gum and wore an enormous feather boa, as if it was pretending to be Çoki. We drove it away from the zoo with pitchforks and torches. Good thing it was afraid of fire. I cannot believe none of you heard about this."

Awkward silence. The group did not know whether she was serious or insane.

Arpita did not think Clarisse was bonkers but understood why the story was a bombshell to the group: Çoki scattered her ÇD Anon members among cottages outside town, fearful their interaction with official Çokland citizens and cast members might disrupt what she had taken so long to nurture. In fact, she lodged Clarisse in a forest, but her addict cravings were so pertinacious she applied for the high school's vacant media arts position. The school chose her over Tabitha. Experience. Clarisse had once been a guidance counselor – at an anime camp. Tabitha obtained the other vacant position: Principal.

Clarisse's days were predictable. She taught several hours in the morning, then devoted eight hours to trolling online. Until yesterday's disaster. Classes resumed this morning on the soccer field, everyone in thick winterwear. Clarisse handed out construction paper and crayons. Henceforth, Principal Tabitha announced, Clarisse would teach *mixed* media arts – not a decision Alfred received lightly. "Tell me, Tabitha, how is this different than art class?" Because the photocopier was demolished, Clarisse's students spent the morning drawing missing person leaflets. The likeness of a pink dwarf bear with an emerald headscarf and feather boa crowned each leaflet.

Give her credit, Arpita thought. Clarisse was forthright about her addiction. How she survived the present loss of Internet was a mystery, but Arpita foresaw no path for her redemption. Clarisse's trolling was insatiable. As for Arpita, she knew she would never return to Boston, not in this life (her parents somehow still believed in reincarnation). The cottage by the lake was Arpita's permanent home – with its crafts, absence of electronics, and long walks along the lake – hip flask at hand.

Josh broke the silence. "Arpita. You're his neighbor. How is Teller handling this?"

Arpita recalled the name on the mailbox and shrugged. "Uh, I have never met him. Why?"

"Well, he must be hurting. He owns all the property in the monster, I mean storm's wake. I assure you, not everyone is insured." Josh was a CPCU (certified property casualty underwriter) in real life, an actuary, the most boring occupation Arpita could imagine. She was surprised he was a Çok Dilli addict and not a drunk. Arpita admonished herself. The brilliant PhD candidate was the drunkard, not the CPCU.

Clarisse again. "Mr. Teller posted a sign by the high school debris site saying, 'Stop the Steal'. Tabitha heard he is furious the town is rebuilding the school without public debate. He claims it is unconstitutional – a violation of the Fourth Amendment's prohibition of unreasonable search and seizure."

Inga raised her hand. "Ich... I are nur 'ne Anwältin (Entsḥuldigung) Juristin in Kiel (dat's in Germany). I tinke, Herr Teller mehbee confuse. Die fünf... Fifde Amendment spielt here – das tackeeng des privat properteys by 'ner government for n'öffentlichen purpose. Ich tinke, dat die relevante phrase 'Eminent Domain' ist. Die Government müst nur 'Just Compensation' zeig... show. Vervee klar?"

Clarisse smiled graciously, ignored Inga's interruption, and continued.

"Tabitha says Mr. Teller wants to build a hotel casino. He says it will put Çokland on the map, raise property values for everyone. Of course, we are already on a map and the townspeople do not own any property. He does. So, the town board voted unanimously for rebuilding the school."

Arpita waited five seconds, then interjected. "Can we get back to Çoki? Have the missing person flyers turned up anything?"

Silence.

"Well, have any of us seen him since the last time we got together? Anyone?"

A Ryan Gosling lookalike raised his hand. He wore cargo pants and a Barbie t-shirt – an obvious recent 'recruit.' He began sheepishly, tugging at the duvet he draped above his shoulders.

"I skated past the school last week. You know, just acquainting myself with the digs, and this chick, I mean officer, in a patrol car with an undercut flashes her siren and tells me to slow down; I might hit one of the children."

Arpita surveyed the impatient stares.

"Well, the fuchsia bear, Çoki, was sitting next to her, talking to the dispatcher – wearing a badge!"

The stares were no longer impatient. They were intent – not much of a distinction in Çok Dilli's language courses, but a crucial one for the audience.

"And a forest green cap. Goofy! I mean, come on, who wears a forest green cap over an emerald headscarf?"

Josh: "Uh, I think the headscarf is mandatory. It's not her fault the uniform clashes." Josh wore a bright orange parka over vintage raspberry ski pants. He was a fan of sartorial distinction.

Arpita tried to push the discussion back on track. "So, what did Çoki say? To the dispatcher? To anyone?"

"Not much. Besides, I think Çoki is mute. I haven't even heard her growl. Have any of you?"

Several headshakes.

"She did, however, float some text bubbles – perhaps 'Not Dad!' and 'Not again!', but I can't be sure. To be honest, I was a lot more interested in her partner. She's a hot..."

Multiple stern glares silenced him.

"What? You can't blame me for trying. It is so lonely by the lake."

Please God, thought Arpita, *make this a different lake!*

"So, how do we get home, anyway?"

"Well," volunteered Josh, "the same way we arrived. I have been back twice. Both times the pink bear judged me ready, returned to me to my property-casualty world in Cleveland, then bingo, I returned. Just because I racked up ÇPs instead of driving down combined ratios. Until we find her, I will be hosting hiking tours up a cardboard mountain."

Arpita turned back to the Ryan Gosling lookalike. "That's it? You tried to shag Çoki's partner and that's all. Çoki just sat there?"

"No, no, of course not. She exited the patrol car, told Liz (that's her name, Officer Liz) to keep watch while she fetched donuts. She padded off in the direction of the lake. I wanted to tell her the donut shop was the other way, but I'm new here. I assume she knew a better place. I waited until the bear was long out of sight before I shagged Officer Liz. Not a bad town. I kind of like it here."

Universal reactions of disgust.

The meeting eventually adjourned, and Arpita returned for 'last call' at the bar. The evening newscast extolled the incredible response of the fire and police departments to the previous day's disaster, then cut to bulldozers clearing the school grounds. A septuagenarian in a blue suit and red tie picketed in the background.

SIXTEEN

"C'mon, Jacques, she is just having fun."

"It is not within her scope of responsibilities."

"*Scope of responsibilities?* Do you hear yourself? She is a living, thinking being, with a precocious child's personality and imagination. She likes dolls, old fashioned horror films, and make-believe. Not every unit is as smart, sophisticated, and glamorous as your secret heartthrob, Jacques."

Jacques jolted.

"What? You don't think we see it?"

Jacques seethed. He began to reply but was cut short.

"Relax, man. It is not like any of this is real. I go home each night to my stereo, Spotify, and pet cockatoo. You go home to, what, your books?"

A veiled insult? Jacques could not decide.

"Don't quibble, Jacques. I'm not as articulate as you, and neither of us has time for another long-winded parable from the old days."

The old days! Jacques winced but resisted the temptation to rise and stomp off. Jacques felt guilty of many things, but seldom of making a scene. Twenty-five years of marriage cured him. Cory's accusation was to some extent accurate. Jacques' sessions with Mirva resembled the platonic side of marriage, but he left it behind every evening.

"The Girls – and I mean all of them – need occasional playtime. What Marielle is doing is harmless."

"Harmless? She frightened the Bejesus out of that group of hikers."

"Yeah? So what! They raced home, told everyone the Abominable Snowman or Yeti (*They could not even agree!*) was on the loose, and weekend adventurers stormed the area looking for clues, trying to prove or debunk the legend. Was anyone injured? No. Traumatized? No. The local businesses love the surge in tourism, even if the fire department spends a ridiculous amount of time rescuing lost hikers."

"What about the monster sightings at the lake? How does that assist the swim camps?"

"It is the middle of winter, Jacques. A couple sightings? The camps will reopen in June, right on schedule. The only difference is, there will be a wait list to enroll. I know it has been a while, Jacques, but try to remember childhood. Do you remember how cool it was to go to someplace spooky?"

Jacques remembered spelunking with his friends, daring each other to proceed without their headlamps. He remembered sneaking onto cornfields, swiping the choicest ears, then being chased through the maze by an old hound dog and its shotgun-toting owner. He remembered camping by a lake under the stars. His parents read ghost stories until long after midnight, acting out the parts with their hands silhouetted against the tent's canvas. He would set a toy boat afloat, carrying a lone Chinese lantern, on its journey to the Styx. The flutter of ducks rising to meet the dawn persuaded him the boat arrived safely.

Cory continued. "The swim camps will be fine. I'll bet you a dollar the local newspaper posts a bounty for anyone who delivers photographic proof of the beast. The problem – known only to us programmers – is that Marielle can jam their cameras and manipulate the images. She has a more imaginative eye for art than any machine in the AI universe. The kids will think they have captured the beast live, but when they scroll through their photos and videos, all they will find are menacing cloud formations reflected on the lake's surface."

"What I am saying is Marielle tries hard to play discreetly, to not disturb the adults, but when there is a witness, she manipulates the evidence, so the witness looks blind, confused, or foolish. If that is what it takes to keep her motivated, I am all for it."

Jacques was not convinced. Cory evidently saw.

"Okay, Papi, what's Mirva's secret? She must feel the pressure. They all do. Heck, you told me just yesterday she resents the mundane stuff, that she seemed depressed."

Jacques could not disagree. He shrugged.

"What is her outlet? How does she cope, keep from detonating?"

Jacques thought hard before answering.

"That is our role, Cory. That is why you and I are still employed."

Quizzical look.

"We all write decent code. But the best coders? Anton sacked them. What sets us apart is we are also good therapists – not language mavens, not first-in-class programmers, but therapists – guys who somehow draw the best out of our units. We make them feel real, make them appreciate how important they are to us, make them want to make us (you and me *personally*) proud. That is why Marielle adores you."

Cory objected. "I wouldn't go that far. We are more like childhood BFFs."

"Whatever works. Mirva does not go berserk, because she has someone she can trust and confide in – every day, like clockwork. Support means someone she can relate and talk to."

"And you don't think Marielle talks to me? That's all she does. Humming, singing, blabbing about this or that, regaling me with her doll stories. The personality breakthrough was about three months ago. She couldn't wait to blurt it out. She galloped past a couple trick-or-treaters as the Headless Horseman but laced their Snickers bars with THC. They returned home agitated and excited, but also visibly high, so their parents thought they hallucinated. So clever! So creative!

I am telling you, Jacques, we can't steal their childhoods. They need to mature at their own pace."

Jacques sought compromise. "I hear you, Cory. Addams Family cosplay is not the problem. It is the fallout from too-frequent public sightings. She needs to be a lot more discreet."

"We are ten steps ahead of you. She promised to limit her cosplay (*I like that description. Thank you!*) to the forested sections of the Teller Estate. The estate is surrounded by fence – once electrified, but recently unplugged at the behest of the fire marshal, and there are *No Trespassing* signs everywhere. The only person she risks frightening is a septuagenarian former colleague of ours who should not be in that world in the first place! Let him be frightened. He knows it isn't real."

"For your sake and mine, I hope you are correct."

Jacques separated the recyclable and compostable matter and placed the tray on the cart. He was grateful his next session was with Helen and not Mirva. Too soon!

SEVENTEEN

Donatello was shrewd. Myaing gave him credit. Erecting a wall along the southern and western shores months before Çokland was developed was prescient. He knew Çok Dilli Corporation's founders personally. He knew they planned a gentrified online "university" environment (as indeed are most brick-and-mortar universities) that insulated its observers (the company's online students) from such culturally edifying inconveniences as different skin color, caste discrimination, poverty, and eye shape. On the other hand, the founders wanted to project an image of progressivity, especially on matters of religion, gender, and sexual preference. So, the company ticked off the boxes but, except for black and white, never broached race nor the socio-economic divide. Those were presumably bridges too far.

Donatello's wall was not entirely physical. He apparently could not find enough razor wire. So, he scattered naval mines off the coast, thousands of them, deterring anyone beyond the western and southern shores from immigrating. This ensured the property he scooped up in town remained desirable, and that his neighbors' appearance did not affront him.

Myaing wondered how and why a distant shore even existed, or how it came to be populated, but recalled the company invested heavily in artificial intelligence. The AI engines had evidently been busy filling in details the original Çok Dilli modelers "inadvertently" left out – *e.g.*, the presence of multiple continents, of vast oceans, of different races to the west and south, and of extreme poverty, cruelty, and unrest in most of the non-western world. Unbeknownst to Çok Dilli Corporation's C-Suite, its AI engines were just doing their job. If they had feelings, they probably felt proud. "Won't Sami and Anton be impressed!"

Myaing thought about the border fencing and naval mines. She once met the self-proclaimed Donatello. She attended a soiree for Çok Dilli Corporation's hundreds of unpaid volunteers, hosted at the company's swank new headquarters in Albany. That was, what, six years ago? She begged a hairstylist client to borrow suitable attire. The 60-something lawyer lent her a charcoal pinstripe dress suit, black pumps, and white cotton shirt with button-down ruffle collar – the same outfit the lawyer wore while interviewing for a Ninth Circuit clerkship in the 1980s. Myaing also borrowed the money for the Greyhound ticket – 4,907 miles of highway each direction. She ached afterward for a week.

The lawyer found the suit and outfit in the back of her closet. They no longer fit but would definitely fit the young hairdresser. The suit was beautifully tailored, albeit slightly moth-eaten, but it proved hopelessly out of place among Çok Dilli Corporation's zealously casual hipsters. Myaing tugged at her pantyhose, another sartorial fail, and hid behind the table of hors d'oeuvres. She stuffed her knockoff Tumi computer bag with goodies for her family – a full meal's worth for each member, then teetered unsteadily to the dessert table. Heeled shoes with pointed toes were not her forte.

That is when she spied the guy – the guy who somehow transported himself to Çok Dilli Corporation's animated cyberworld and set about mucking up the works. The only reason she noticed him was he was the only other attendee in a suit. He wore a navy pinstripe, the same vintage as her own, and he himself appeared of comparable vintage to the lawyer whose clothes Myaing borrowed. The man had evidently consumed a few pastries in his day and was consuming one of them then.

She watched his routine: Spot a new face – female – then attempt small talk, typically a long-winded joke without a punchline, then shake his head as the quarry melted into the crowd. She noticed something else. The fellow never approached her, nor any women of color. He looked through or beyond them, as if they didn't exist. Myaing had seen enough. She had met his type before. Perhaps all the executives – even the ones in jeans and chinos – felt similarly. Had she not herself been deposited in this cartoon world, she would never have remembered his face.

Myaing was a Myanmar refugee in the real world, the one comprised of atoms, who financed night classes in Vancouver with what remained from styling hair and nails and driving a taxi, after contributing her share to her extended family's living expenses. Her parents thanked Allah for emigrating before the military reasserted control, but she secretly blamed him for the brother, uncle, and countless friends lost in the conflict.

Myaing discovered Çok Dilli within days of landing on Canadian soil and developed passable English. An irrepressible sense of gratitude impelled her to volunteer her rare moments of "free time" as a contributor to Çok Dilli's Burmese and Thai language courses. Myaing invested what remained of her emotion (being a refugee deadened most of it) in building and improving the Burmese course, and in browbeating anyone who would listen that Çok Dilli should base some of its stories and cartoon teaching characters on Far Eastern cultures. She also lobbied furiously for Rohingya but never secured approval.

Myaing was devasted when her childhood idol, Aung San Suu Kyi, stood idle while the Burmese Army massacred her former neighbors, then defended those actions at the International Court of Justice. Çok Dilli worsened her frayed mind in 2021, when the company announced it was "mothballing" Burmese development, and that her services were no longer required. She stewed at home, guzzling faluda which she brewed downstairs in her parents' bubble tea shop, watching the bathroom scale register every ounce. Her online tirades and letters to executives went unanswered. The thinly veiled death threats didn't help.

It was after one such overly transparent missive that she found herself deposited on a chair in a circle with eleven strangers who shared her obsession with Çok Dilli Corporation and its services. Unlike the others in attendance, Çoki Bear did not beam her to the familiar cyberworld of Hami, Midori, Liz and Lucie, but to a dilapidated mountainside hut in Çokland's northernmost frontier. Myaing's reward for her unwavering Çok Dilli devotion? Solitary confinement in cartoon land.

She was not entirely alone. Pixar-like caricatures of hikers and shepherds passed her way, reciting lines from one Çok Dilli course or another, but no one with substance, and certainly no one from the real-world circle of chairs in Vancouver, ventured in her direction.

The punishment gnawed at her. Sure, d'Hein and Holzkrall could have called the FBI. Deportation to death or lifelong slavery would have been the result. Instead, the cheery pink dwarf bear intervened with what she evidently thought was a better solution. No friends, no family, indefinite incarceration, and no way to communicate with the outside world. Myaing couldn't even scratch days on the wall. *What is the point of counting if you don't know what you are counting down from?* "Thank you, Çoki," she seethed. "You are a doll. I would rip your heart out and stuff you, except you never had one, did you? A heart. You have always had stuffing."

Her outlook improved the day she met Josh, a bearded trail guide with mutton chop sideburns and Evgeni Plushenko mullet, who was leading a Pixar-like group of weekend adventurers up a cardboard mountain. Myaing knew instantly he was from the real world, as mysteriously transported here as she. She nearly tackled him to make his acquaintance.

The two met frequently. It turned out there were dozens of ÇD Anon members in Çokland. All were there to wean themselves of their obsession – some permanently, others, like Josh, to check in temporarily. He told her about being an actuary in Cleveland. Myaing resolved, when she returned home, to make actuarial science her major. She admired the field's comfort with uncertainty. She'd learned early in life to accept heaping servings of happenstance, fuzzy logic, and random bad luck (Exhibit A: her presence here; Exhibit B: being born Rohingya during a time of civil strife). Josh explained what mattered to an actuary was intuiting the shape of underlying distributions controlling uncertain future events, computing associated probabilities, then employing those computations to competitive advantage. Of course, Josh was talking about the frequency and severity of burglaries, house fires, and car accidents, but the concepts were universal. Nothing in life was predictable, just estimable.

Myaing liked Josh. He had no reserve. She peppered him with questions, and he shared everything he knew. She came to know more about Çokland than its own townspeople ever bothered to learn. Josh explained, for example, that there were several Çokland characters who were invested with more than superficial personalities. Their names were already familiar to Myaing. Alfred, Elsie, Midori, Hami, Buddy, Skipper, Liz, Tabitha, Zagreet, Adya and the talking sea lion with the blue scarf, Balthazar, were the principal characters in all the Çok Dilli language courses, but Myaing did not know they actually existed and had not yet met them. Josh could not decide if they were 100 percent programmed or had thoughts and dreams of their own. They certainly behaved autonomously, like the mysterious pink dwarf bear, but bore no evident awareness of a world outside their own.

Myaing tried on occasion to attend ÇD Anon meetings in town, if only to broaden her social network, but was rebuffed within minutes of departure by a sleuth of Crayola-colored dwarf bears (sage, teal, saffron, and mauve, but never pink), which steered her back to her cabin. Except for Myaing's attempted forays into town, the bears kept their distance.

"Such a dumb cabal!" she recalled remarking. "Why doesn't Çoki ever show himself?" Myaing meant "dumb" in the literal sense. Josh explained it had a figurative meaning, one which perhaps better reflected her feelings. At the time, she just meant their method of communication – floating text bubbles that communicated intended utterances, provided you could read them. Those night classes in Vancouver helped a lot. So did her online English classes with Çok Dilli Corporation. Myaing repented.

Myaing's feelings toward Josh were evidently mutual because he dropped by frequently. He taught her what he had learned about cybernetic mountaineering and survival skills, brought her groceries from town ("No more roughing it!"), and shared stories about growing up in Cleveland. He agreed to accompany her the day she decided to circumnavigate Çokland's four shores on foot.

Çokland was surprisingly small. The entire journey lasted three months. Josh declared it was modeled after Middle Earth, not Westeros. Myaing had been to neither Middle Earth nor Westeros, just Vancouver, and therefore could not disagree. It was on their journey together that Josh and Myaing learned about the border fencing and naval mines defending the western and southern shores.

Scattered along the perimeter were occasional refugee outposts and encampments – settled by real-world Çok Dilli linguists who were ushered there after venting their outrage too expressively to Çok Dilli executives when their favorite offering was reworked or cancelled, or their hard-won trophies were revoked.

Myaing met one guy, several years her junior, whose first infraction was swatting the mother of a teacher who sequestered his phone for making forum posts during class. The crazy thing was, Herman was posting in the Burmese language channel. Herman could not even say maingalarpar ("hello"), much less spell it (မင်္ဂလာပါ). The crazier thing was that Çoki rehabilitated him on the outskirts of Çokville, with the same roaming and access privileges as Josh. Myaing only sent letters – nasty, threatening ones, but only letters. She never called a Swat team on anyone.

Herman's second offense was more serious. He was now an outcaste, like Myaing, surviving alone on an inhospitable beach rather than alone on an inhospitable mountainside. Herman evidently kept his word. He forbore trolling the Çok Dilli Community Forum and began taking lessons seriously. Too seriously. Sometime after Myaing "left" Vancouver, Çok Dilli introduced something called leagues to motivate commitment. There was the American League, the National League, the Grapefruit League, and the Cactus League. Beyond the various baseball leagues were the food leagues – ones which matched the hierarchy of alimentary cravings of the company's ursine mascot: Honeypot League; Ranger Smith Sandwich League; and so forth. Herman spent 87 weeks in the Coho

Salmon League – the highest league, the one colored salmon in honor of the company's mascot. Like most high achievers, Herman depended on occasional double ÇP bonus minutes (typically, 15 or 30) to pad his total and remain astride the top echelon of achievers.

The dependence changed around week 85. Herman hit a milestone, received a congratulatory promise from Çoki herself that 15 minutes of double ÇPs were forthcoming and then... nothing. Ten ÇPs per exercise, not twenty. The first couple times this happened, Herman shrugged off the slight as a glitch. By the fifth or sixth phony prize announcement, Herman knew the slights were intentional. Some geek at Çok Dilli was handicapping acknowledged achievers to make up for their own lackluster effort, or this was Çoki Bear's own sick attempt at humor.

Myaing proffered a third possibility: a misguided psychology experiment – part of the company's perverted X-Y testing.

Whatever the reason, Herman reacted predictably. He returned to the forum, posted withering criticisms of Çok Dilli and its management on every social medium on the planet, and publicly doxed the founders and top executives. Where he unearthed their social security numbers remains a mystery, but the FBI did not have time to investigate. Çoki swept Herman to a secluded beach edged with barbed wire three days shy of his eighteenth birthday. Herman, like the other Çok Dilli outcasts she met, was not especially fond of the pink bear, nor of his multi-colored sleuth of mute enforcers.

Darker secrets lurked beyond Çokland's perimeter.

Rumor circulated among the encampments, especially those bordering the western and southern shores, of boatloads of computer-animated beings, turned away by the defensive barriers, or capsized by cybernetic waves. All manner of flotsam found its way past the fencing and littered the beaches – empty suitcases, articles of clothing, a child's doll. Myaing kept copious mental note of whom she met, whom she came to trust, and the detritus from thwarted landings.

The three-month journey was an eye opener for Josh, too, but Myaing kept her thoughts to herself. As much as she admired Josh, she could not bring herself to trust him. He caromed back and forth from the real world, deposited here only during lapses in self-control. Unlike Myaing, he could go anywhere and communicate freely with anyone. It was, as he described, a cozy, laid-back, cost-free detox facility.

For example, Josh did not think anything of the razor wire or naval mines. "National defense. Who knows what lurks out there, waiting to invade and pillage us?"

Nor did he associate the debris along the shoreline with capsized boats of refugees. "All these encampments. I know you like these people, but they should be more conscientious about the environment. Just because there isn't a carting service, does not mean they should throw their junk in the ocean. Dig a hole! Make a landfill!"

Josh did not even see a problem with the dwarf bear mafia blocking her access to town. "It is for everyone's good. Until they realize your death threat letters were idle tantrums, they and the community are fearful. You would expect no less in the real world."

"Listen," he said. "You are a born actuary – someone who grasps uncertainty. No one *expects* you to do something rash (the most likely event), but to the extreme right of that expected inaction are a host of actions that remain highly plausible (*i.e.*, nonzero probability) and severely hurtful. The community needs time to believe the odds of a physical attack on anyone or anything are *negligible*. Give them a few more months. They will see. Meanwhile, let's clean up this litter. This beach would be a great place to lead one of my adventure tours, but the garbage everywhere is a turn-off."

Myaing was grateful Josh did not mention "fat tails" during his actuarial discourse or exhort her to render Çoki's perception of her "fat tail" less so. She hated the phrase, always suspecting a double entendre, always inspecting herself afterward in the mirror.

Myaing and Josh completed their circumnavigation in late autumn. Certain evenings, when Josh was off guiding an excursion, she would pull the shades, light a fire, and entertain other *ex-patriate* Earthlings who had become indefinite captives along Çokland's perimeter. Far from assuaging their frayed nerves, cyberspace exile provoked them. Their thoughts were more violent than ever. No stranger to juntas, Myaing lobbied for a coup.

Çokland was gentrified, she reasoned, and that was its principal weakness. Myaing characterized its citizens and creators as "pansies".

She pointed to Çok Dilli's French turnpike – ten massive Autobahns with 200 regional markers – and took roll call of its subjects. Politics? *Here!* Crime? *Here!* Military tactics and warfare? *Silence.* Ditto the German turnpike, Italian turnpike and presumably most others. She recalled a bit of military history in the Russian course but the course, like its motherland, had become a pariah. The founders of Çokland had gone out of their way to distance themselves as far as possible from military matters and were therefore militarily defenseless. The closest Çokland came to securing its borders was unwittingly relying on Donatello's pecuniary self-interest in keeping out "undesirables."

"Won't Çok Dilli be surprised," Myaing mused, "when we take everything by force."

EIGHTEEN

Arctic chill confronted Midori as she lifted the sash and hoisted Hami in. 2:30 am sharp. Hami was punctual.

The amateur detectives gathered their equipment and tiptoed downstairs to the back kitchen door. If they hurried, they could reach the Teller estate by three. A waning crescent moon lay low over the hazy eastern horizon. They counted on the moon's rising to light their way.

Ten days of unexplained havoc propelled them. Everything pointed to Çoki Bear or, rather, her mysterious disappearance eight days prior. First, there was the feather Skipper discovered six days ago in the Teller estate forest. Hami and Midori's subsequent late-night fact-finding mission ended abruptly but not unfruitfully. Discarded candy wrappers attested Skipper's account. Something happened in that forest! They just needed to steel themselves against the wildlife to determine what.

Five days ago, a skyscraper-sized monster ploughed through town, crushing their school, proclaiming itself Çoki, despite sharing no resemblance to the cuddly dwarf bear, save its pink fur and choice of oversized accoutrements. The fact that it spoke, rather than lofted text bubbles, was evidence enough the beast was an imposter. Perhaps more suspicious was the admonition by town leaders to recharacterize its destructive wake as an act of nature. *As if!* Only the newscasters acquiesced. Why the attempted deception? What did the town have to gain?

And then there was that phone call – the one they overheard on Labor Day weekend, three short days before classes resumed. Hami itched to know which K-pop acts city hall approved for autumn, and how could she procure tickets? Midori, for her part, could not have cared less. She nevertheless boosted Hami to the correct office window at city hall and climbed in after her. Neither of them expected to hear Adya in the adjacent office. Adya was the baker's wife. She always worked late, and Jagreet always baked her something special.

Adya sounded upset. Really upset. Hami observed the phone on the desk and that one of its buttons was lit. Midori motioned "Quiet", lifted the receiver to their joined heads, then pushed the button.

"Spy on our neighbors? How? Jagreet spends his day baking. And I spend my day arranging permits for your camera crews to interrupt the town's activities. It takes me six days, sometimes seven, to schedule each week. Jagreet and I never complained, not once. But now you are telling me, the town does not really have any activities to interrupt – that our activities are pre-programmed animations, our childhood memories are implanted fiction, and even the film crews are contrived to perpetuate the myth that we are real. For what? To help..."

Adya paused. "Hold on a sec. It is probably nothing, but one of my phone buttons is illuminated. I'll be back in a minute."

Caught! Hami and Midori dropped the receiver and hurtled out the window.

"Phew! That was close. What did I tell you, Midori? Avatars!"

"Avatars," Midori conceded. She and Hami were the only ones who took the monstrously large Çoki imposter in stride.

Thankfully, the devastation occurred on Friday. The town spent the weekend preparing the playing fields for class on Monday. It borrowed circus and bat mitzva tents from Heaven knows where and plugged in what must have been five hundred space heaters. Even in Çokland, superstores and Amazon were everywhere.

If only that were all! Midori was inclined to shrug it off. But a cleaning lady set fire to herself on Saturday, a janitor on Sunday. Townspeople rushed to book cleaning dates on Monday, fearful all the maids and janitors would be dead by Tuesday. It was not merely cleaning ladies and janitors. Hami and Midori found their ghost-exorcising business backlogged, not because anyone sensed heightened paranormal activity, nor saw the fliers Skipper idly promised to post around town in exchange for advance wages, but because the duo's patented Eureka ghost sweeper sucked up dust along with carpet-bound spirits. The art connoisseur Alfred and school principal Tabitha vouched wholeheartedly for its effectiveness.

Events grew weirder. Rumors circulated that a dragon-like serpent occupied the still-unfrozen center of the lake, an area previously reserved for non-migrating geese. Hikers reporting spotting the Yeti. Both girls wished they had been there.

Yet Hami and Midori's biggest concern, aside from avoiding frostbite at school, was dodging the increasingly erratic behavior of townspeople. It was as if, one by one, they woke from a trance and began questioning their daily routines. A garage mechanic repaired the fender of a late-model SUV and drove off – sans explanation to his wife or the owner. Officer Liz inaugurated her first-ever investigation – auto theft – scouring the Internet for YouTube advice on how to track down stolen vehicles, and consulting with Skipper, the world's leading expert on the video game *Petit Theft Matchbox*.

It was not, alas, Officer Liz's only case. Brawls broke out in nearly every bar and tavern within Çokland. Previously, patrons imbibed, caroused politely, and nodded off and snored when overly inebriated. No longer. Now, a sizable percentage of patrons argued vociferously and threw punches to drive home their insistence. Officer Liz issued more "disturbing the peace" citations in a week than Çokland recorded during its entire previous history. Hami and Midori found an old action figure in Elsie's attic two nights earlier and pulled on the cord. "Someone poisoned the water hole!" rang out. "Exactly!" they exclaimed. And now they were searching for clues.

Hami rued burglarizing Elsie's apartment, not merely because it contained nothing of value, but because it made tonight Hami's turn to lift Midori. The two weekend burglaries were also a bust. First, they targeted the apartment of the drummer who once conned them into selling concert t-shirts outside the concert hall where his band performed – supervised *by his girlfriend*. Hami found the experience humiliating – hoodwinked by yet another impossible-odds prospective boyfriend and future husband! Midori made the best of the situation, overcharging customers when the girlfriend wasn't looking, and pocketing several CDs to catch up on what they missed during the concert. All they found in the drummer's apartment were old socks and photos of classmates. First was Carmelita, the prettiest girl in school, then Erika, Barbara, Marie, and Natascha from Novosibirsk. Under the photos he scribbled a note:

> Mama, was ist mit mir los?
> Frauen gegenüber bin ich willenlos
> Völlig willenlos

"Just think, Hami, if your surname were Meyer, you'd be up there, too."

"Eww," mouthed Hami. They left with the CDs of the drummer's apparent idol, some old geezer in a fedora.

The next evening, they broke into the managing agent's office at the theater, thinking they could secure keys to see the band from one of the unreserved sky boxes. Foiled again. The door from the office into the theater's back corridors was latched from the corridor side. Worse, the managing agent installed baffles to block out the sound. They departed with only two items of value, the as-yet unpublished schedule of upcoming concerts and the contact information for each act's agent. Hami and Midori spent the evening firing off email requests for signed posters, photos, and memorabilia for launching advance publicity. They set up an anonymous P.O. box several months prior for a similar caper.

Hami grasped the fence with both hands and grunted as Midori climbed atop her shoulders to pull herself over. Midori landed with a soft thud. A shovel and miscellaneous equipment narrowly missed her. Hami appeared moments later, thoroughly muddied, after locating her familiar crawl space. She took a moment to shed the yellow fisherman's rain slicker and sou'ester she "borrowed" from the drama department's planned production of *Death Rattle Dazzle*. Hami hung the muddied oilskin and hat on a peg she fashioned from the fence and a twig, and the sleuths set off. "Sleuth" was a heteronym and irony, Hami exclaimed, since their quarry was herself a member of a sleuth. Roleplaying for Çok Dilli Corporation, Hami learned all about heteronyms, homophones, and false cognates. Midori shuddered at the pun and her friend's attempts at humor. She predicted another long evening.

Twenty minutes passed. Hami spied something yellow and brown in the moonlight. They crept forward, secreting themselves behind trees after every step. It was the drama department's hat, pants and slicker. It was the fence they climbed previously. "You said you remembered the coordinates. We are back where we started."

"Easy Hami. These are the coordinates. See?"

Sure enough. The coordinates on the GPS tracker matched those she recorded previously using SimpleNote.

"Something is guiding us in a circle. Let's try again but skip the tracker. Footprints. We haven't had snow in a week. It should not be hard to retrace our path."

Progress was slow but certain. They reached the clearing, the discarded candy wrappers, the old stump, and... a clump of downy green feathers! Midori dropped to her knees and rummaged in the oversized rucksack. She removed the miniature battery-operated leaf blower and set to work. Just as their superannuated Eureka sucked spirits (and dust) out of carpets, their leaf blower separated recently scattered leaves, soil, and debris from foliage that was frozen to the tundra. Their plan was to detect areas where the surface had been recently disturbed. They were also hopeful the noise would keep wildlife at bay – curious, perhaps, but at bay.

Lighting was decent; the crescent moon cast a somber glow. And the leaf blower worked as advertised. But the girls grew disheartened. The boars had contaminated the crime scene, if indeed there was one. Tusks had ground away every inch of the forest floor, probing for insects and soft roots. Nary a sapling remained near the clearing. Leaves and debris scattered wherever she blew. Midori silenced the blower.

"Boared."

"Bored? How can you be bored? We just started? What *is* that?"

Midori heard it, too, the distinctive crackle of a bonfire. Then, the cackle of old voices.

"Double, double toil and trouble; Fire burn and caldron bubble."

Hami pointed to the smoke rising from the trees beyond one side of the clearing and motioned Midori to exit in the opposite direction. They crept away, until they could no longer hear voices, and until the forest grew impenetrable with tall trees and underbrush. They must be near the lake, they reasoned, where the groves which stood sentry resembled original forest – 80 to 100 feet tall, trunks as wide as small cars. A narrow winding footpath improved their gait, transporting them to a small garden and gingerbread cottage. A stovepipe jutted from the thatched roof and billowed smoke. Someone lifted a roller shade. The light from within bathed the girls in a welcoming glow. An old woman thrust open the door and beckoned them inside.

"Hurry girls! The wolves are a'prowl." The girls lurched back at the silhouette's appearance, but Midori steadied Hami, pointing to her ears. Sure enough, the girls heard the howl of wolves, and decided without words to accept the silhouette's invitation.

The interior blinded the girls, but their eyes soon feasted on the furniture, furnishings, and décor.

"So much candy! Everything resembles gingerbread, candy canes, and bonbons."

"Not resembles, my dear yellow girl. Is! And you, sullen green companion? Are you not impressed by my feats of confectionary architecture?"

Midori was as dumbfounded as Hami, just congenitally unreadable. Inwardly, she recoiled at the old woman's features. *Old hag* was a compliment. "Wh...Why would you build a cottage out of candy? On Mr. Teller's estate?

"He is a queer one, is he not? Goodies for when he is peckish, I suppose. Edacious appetite, he has. Why, he devoured a week's worth of scones in one sitting. Would you like one?" Hami nodded but Midori glared reproval.

"That is very kind, Ma'am, but who are you? You have evidently been here a while, yet I have never seen you in town, nor ever heard mention of a tenant on Mr. Teller's property."

The woman set a heaping plate of scones, jam, and fruit before Hami. Hami had already accepted a seat at the dining table. "Who am I? That was your first question, was it not?"

Midori nodded.

"Hard to say, that is. Not many of us have names around here. More like functions: the gardener, the postman, the mayor, and, until recently, the police officer. It is easier, I suppose, for those of you with names. Less to remember. Still, I would like to think I have one. Let me think."

"There was this fellow, Engelbert Humperdinck – no, not the crooner. The crooner was a namesake. The original Engelbert Humperdinck was a German composer – late nineteenth century. He mentioned me in passing in one of his operas; called me Rosina Leckermaul, although I am no more a raisin nor sweet-tooth than your yellow-garmented friend. If he saw me today, he would probably call me Prunella. I am not sure Jacob and Wilhelm – my real parents – would approve either name. The point is, I have no name, just a function. And my function is to tend a gingerbread house in the only large forest near town. Please, try a scone." Hami showed no sign of poisoning, so Midori accepted.

1890s? Gay parents? The incongruity intensified Midori's unease, but the hag's scones were delicious, and Midori was famished. She decided to engage in small talk.

"These pastries are perfect, delicious. Don't you agree, Hami?"

Hami nodded approval. Her mouth was too full to speak.

"And I see you have a vegetable garden in the summer." She recalled stepping over the frozen cabbages when she entered. "But is that all you eat, candies and pastries?"

"It seems boring, does it not? To be honest, it is horrible for my teeth and my figure." The hag grinned, displaying a row of crooked, decayed, and half-missing teeth. "But money is short, and Mr. Teller does not take kindly to poaching – not that I am spry enough to catch a wild boar. So, yes, I content myself with flour and sugar until some lost creature wanders in my door – slow, small, and trusting enough to thrust into the oven." The hag cackled. "As if that ever happens!"

Midori started at the laugh. Hami continued munching.

"Immigration policy. Çokland has it all wrong." Hami stopped chewing, suddenly interested.

"Well," continued the hag, "I am not from these parts. My original cottage was in the Black Forest. The closest city is Freiburg. I do not suppose either of you have been to Freiburg?"

Dumb stares.

"Of course, not. You would only venture there for cuckoo clocks, and who needs a cuckoo clock nowadays? You have cell phones. Well, the townspeople were nasty beasts. They accused me of stealing children. Me. Can you believe it? They drove me away with pitchforks, the same way you drove away that dwarf bear imposter. It took me decades to find this forest, and desperate pleading to persuade Mr. Teller to let me stay, but here I am, ready and willing to contribute to my adoptive homeland. But Çokland, it seems, is not ready to accept my contribution. Too old? Too wizened? For whatever reason, I do not fit the desired profile. So, here am I, tucked away in a forest. No safety net, no social services, no protein, just a few sacks of flour and sugar which I bought with the proceeds from a dozen purloined cuckoo clocks."

Midori watched Hami's eyes well with tears. *Stop it, Hami! That's infectious.* Midori wiped away her own.

"I am sorry, dearies. I did not mean to sadden you. You, green girl, eat up. And you, yellow girl, help me with the oven. It is just hot enough to prepare my next confection."

Hami rose obediently and followed the old woman several steps to the oven. Hami opened the oven wide, per the woman's instructions, then inquired, "Okay, what's next?"

"Why you, my dear!" And the old woman began pushing Hami into the oven's gaping mouth.

Midori, meanwhile, caught sight of the sack of flour in the corner. *Genetically modified grain!* She spit out the remains of the scone and turned to alert Hami just as the old woman divulged her true intentions. "Run!" she screamed, as Midori's shovel crashed down on the skull of the hostess.

NINETEEN

Dense fog rose from the Mohawk and settled over the isthmus to the south. Sami pushed through the doors keeping the mist at bay, paused to greet faces in the vestibule, then found Jacques and Cory at Jacques' workstation. Anton arrived a couple minutes later.

Jacques and Cory evidently stayed late. Very late. Neither changed their wardrobe nor shaved. An unpleasant odor wafted from their direction.

Anton had demurred, but Jacques and Cory were persistent. They lobbied to give Marielle (*aka* Shelly) a second chance. Mirva and the others were working triple-time orchestrating disaster recovery in Çokland, as well as covering for the missing bear's countless ministerial, marketing, and motivational duties. There were no AI units to spare. Jacques promised Anton Marielle was ready.

This morning's report? So far, so good. The package was delivered personally by Jagreet and Adya. The operatives hid in the underbrush until the postman made his usual delivery – a dozen boxes from Amazon and others – then inserted their package in the pile.

The morning in Çokland was cold but glorious. A blinding sun shimmered against the frozen lake surface and roused Arpita from her torpor. She pulled on her leggings, threw a *Where's Waldo* t-shirt over her sports bra, drained the remnant drops from the fifth at her bedside, donned a parka, and began her morning hike around the lake. She spotted Elsie as she turned the corner in front of Mr. Teller's gate.

"Elsie?" Arpita exclaimed. Elsie haunted the exact same bar as Arpita. Everyone there knew Elsie. Heck, everyone in town knew Elsie. She was a celebrated hoodwinker, adventurer, and survivor. Whatever the challenge, Elsie pulled through ... on her terms. Without compromise. Arpita adored her but wondered how the granddaughter endured. Some people make great friends but miserable housemates. Too much energy. Too much personality. Arpita imagined Elsie to be such a personality.

"You have keys to Mr. Teller's estate?" Arpita was not sure if she was incredulous or in awe.

"Want to peek around? It is far too stodgy for my taste, but it positively reeks of wealth. Mrs. Teller hired me to give her a hand."

"*Mrs.* Teller?" This time Arpita's voice betrayed dismay.

"A quiet affair. Last month. Love at first sight, they say, although I hope she is in it for the money. A waste of youth and beauty, otherwise."

"And you... are... helping... her?"

"Mrs. Teller advertised. I answered. I think I am the only one she trusts near her husband. From what I hear, he won't even acknowledge another woman unless she is young enough to be his daughter. It is fortunate he does not have one – for her sake, I mean."

Arpita tried to digest what she heard.

Elsie waved to the man wielding a pickaxe in the garden. "Hi, Buddy, how is it going? Keeping an eye on Skipper, I hope."

Elsie turned to Arpita. "Mel hates it when Skipper noses around the house. I know he is just looking for a place to play *Zombie Underworld*, but Mel is paying him to dig trenches, not play."

"Mel?"

"Mrs. Melliflores Teller. Mel, for short. She says her parents are Rhäto-Romansch, whatever that means. Melliflores apparently means honey flowers, which is redundant, don't you think? To the bees. Or Mr. Teller. As I explained, Mrs. Teller preferred an older assistant. She rejected the first applicant, my granddaughter Liz! Ditto a dozen other young women. Thankfully, Liz found another job, but, what with the tax assessment for the new post office, school, and library, I am grateful Mel is worried about Donny's wandering hands and eyes. I need the money."

"Uh, why are Buddy – that is his name, right? – and his son digging in the garden?"

"Why, to plant things, silly! Mrs. Teller plans a maze of hedges – a place to befuddle Mr. Teller when his libido is aroused, and to thwart the women who come calling. She wants something so grand and complex that even the smartest minds will take an hour to enter and exit. Lesser minds? Well, the dogs will do a weekly sweep for carcasses."

"But it is the middle of winter," Arpita protested. "The ground must be hard as rock."

"That is exactly what Buddy said. That is why he is swinging a pickaxe. I guess she wants to start early. The boxwood is all lined up in the greenhouse."

Arpita furrowed her brow, evidently skeptical.

"My guess is Mr. Teller encouraged her. Married four weeks to the richest man in this corner of the world, and her only expenditures have been the wages of a couple part-time farmhands (Buddy and Skipper), a part-time groundskeeper (me), assorted household appliances, and a greenhouse full of boxwood. No garish trips. No extravagant shopping sprees. Just determination to outbuild the Longleat Maze in Wiltshire. She spends less money than my granddaughter Liz. If you ask me, she is a keeper."

Arpita gazed at Buddy, perspiring heavily in his filthy red gym shorts, head band and hoodie in the middle of January, trying to appear fit and composed, but telescoping exhaustion with every labored stab of the frozen soil. Longleat Maze need not worry, Arpita thought. The Spring planting won't cover a quarter acre.

"Where is Mr. Teller during all this?" inquired Arpita, genuinely curious.

"You missed him. He has a golf cart. Morning exercise, he calls it. He drives to the front gate, loads packages in the cart, then drives back to the mansion. Amazon junk, mostly. Unlike Mel, he is a compulsive shopper. Same blue suit and red tie every day, but underwear? Socks? Shoes? Golf clubs? Lamps? Seat cushions? There must be a dozen boxes a day."

"In any event, I help unload the packages from the golf cart onto a dolly at the house, then roll it into his dining room. There, I line the packages up on an enormous dining table (it must seat 30!). Only then do I come outside to check on Buddy. Mel says Mr. Teller eats his Cocoa Crispies, studies the cereal box, then opens the packages one by one, as if it were Christmas. He is inside now, commencing the dining room half of his morning ritual."

Elsie changed the subject. "Take a walk with me. I have to check the traps."

"Traps?" Arpita's voice registered alarm.

"Well, of course, silly. Mr. and Mrs. Teller don't want anyone snooping around or poaching their prize livestock."

Arpita wondered whether accompanying Elsie on the grounds qualified as snooping. She also wondered whether the livestock had horns. Elsie must have observed the hesitation.

"Oh, don't worry. I know where most of the traps are, I think. I am told they just snap ankles, not sever them. No permanent damage as long as someone finds you. Their property is so vast; it is really hard to hear screams from the house."

Most? Think? No permanent damage? Screams? "Another time, Elsie. I am expected at... at the gym." Arpita struggled to think of an institution that was still intact. The women exchanged pleasantries, Arpita nodded to the man in the filthy red gym shorts, headband, and hoodie (Buddy?) and hastened to the gate at the foot of the driveway. She pulled it shut behind her.

TWENTY

Hunting rifles, makeshift longbows, and pickaxes comprised their arsenal. Myaing assured the seventy assembled insurgents they would need nothing more. Çokland possessed no standing army, had no reservists, and maintained a police force of two – an inexperienced officer named Liz and an unidentified dispatcher. Çokland's only meaningful defense lay to the west and south, along shores they did not intend to cross. Nothing stood between her small infantry and the village to the south except four mute, multi-colored dwarf bears.

Better still, the group would have to trespass or circumnavigate the great Donatello's estate – an obstacle Myaing anticipated with great pleasure.

The dwarf bears were surprisingly absent, and Myaing's infantry made swift progress. They were tired but in good spirits as they camped late afternoon in a dense stand of trees by a frozen lake. Smoke rose from the lone chimney on the other side. Behind the stand of trees stood a fence running the perimeter of a forest – the boundary of the legendary Teller estate. *No Trespassing* signs were posted prominently. Someone located a series of outlets for the recently disconnected electrical fortification and discovered they still worked. The campers huddled around the three portable space heaters Myaing had the foresight to borrow from her cabin, and which the insurgents took turns carrying. Now they took turns dozing, while a handful kept watch.

Reveille sounded at four. The group groped its way in total darkness along the fence, three flashlights in total. Circumnavigation proved harder than foreseen. Time and again, someone tripped over another, slipped on the ice, landed in one creek or another, and emerged bruised, muddied, and wet. The group suffered in the cold. The crescent moon rose and cast indistinct shadows over the cloud-streaked horizon. Myaing proposed a shortcut.

She was the first combatant over the fence, landing with a soft crunch on a frozen snowbank on the other side. The others followed, except for the strongest, stoutest, and fiercest among them – an Oregonian lumberjack in real life – whose broad shoulders supported the others as they reached for the top of the fence and pulled themselves over. The lumberjack searched diligently for an opening but, finding none, wished his comrades success and begged his leave. Myaing watched as he trudged off in the direction whence he came.

Myaing's shrunken infantry took stock of its position. Twelve were soaked and shivering violently. Six hobbled on sprained or twisted ankles. And three massaged severe bruises from falls. They were still several kilometers from town in the middle of a gated forest on one of the coldest nights of the year. Intense grumbling diminished Myaing's sense of mission control. The group crept forward, it hoped, in the direction of Donald Teller's mansion, its first intended destination and, if all proceeded well, the residence of its highest profile hostage.

A pair of high-pitched shrieks froze them in their tracks. "Quick! Duck! Hide!" Myaing commanded, or so she recalled. The truth is, Myaing did not remember what she shouted. She was as shocked and frightened as anyone.

Two muddied apparitions swept past her – one yellow, one green – both shrieking wildly. Such manner of beast Myaing had never encountered. Çokland evidently retained secrets even Josh had not observed. Her mission became more complicated by the minute.

Myaing inhaled the frigid arctic air, exhaled slowly, and summoned her resolve. She yelled, "All clear!" and the insurgents emerged from their respective places of hiding – each grimier, colder, more anxious, and more miserable than before. They continued to edge forward.

Myaing heard a loud crack and an anguished shriek, then another, then another. Three insurgents howled in pain – victims of traps set for… **them**? Fellow combatants rushed to their aid, dislodging the UGG, Doc Marten, and Converse All Star-clad feet from the traps. The three required immediate medical attention, but the enemy lay in wait... anywhere! The group gathered itself into a tight circle, trying desperately to muffle the anguished cry of their fallen comrades and to see what lay ahead in the darkness. The moon penetrated the forest just enough to decry random flickers.

The troop crouched motionless as a rustling grew in the distance. A pair of eyes glistened in the moonlight. Then another. And yet another. The troop abandoned any pretense of soldierly discipline and ran – screaming as they fled. A litter of piglets bounded after them, squealing with delight at being the pursuers rather than the pursued. A couple more traps sprung, a couple more cadets screamed in agony, and the troop found itself scattered along the edge of Donald Teller's expansive front lawn.

A statuary garden fronted the manor house, and various outer structures loomed in the moonlight – a greenhouse, a couple small garden sheds, a stable. The mansion stood somber and quiet. The statuary at the main door deterred them – a lion wielding the shield of Florence to the door's right, a hooded female with raised sword to the door's left, the decapitated head of a bearded victim cradled in her other arm. The group unlatched the stable and tiptoed inside. A pair of old bays eyed them skeptically, snorted, and returned to slumber. The injured combatants threw themselves on hay bales and moaned quietly. The soaked combatants wrapped themselves in horse blankets.

Myaing spotted the golf cart outside and, two at a time, drove her wards quietly down the long driveway to the front gate – the gate by the lake, the same lake where they camped before embarking on their early morning adventure. It was nearly daybreak when she completed the last run, returned the cart, jogged back to her entourage, and latched the gate behind her.

The proprietor of the local tavern expressed delight when so many "fine travelers" burst into his establishment for hot coffee, toddies, and victuals. He was even more delighted when they booked every room upstairs and around back. He summoned the doctor for those who injured themselves hiking and remonstrated them for not wearing sensible hiking boots. "Imagine if you had encountered snakes!"

"Imagine, indeed," thought Myaing. Even in Çokland, snakes hibernated in winter.

An old hag sat humming in the corner. She bore striking resemblance to Famke Janssen's character in *Hansel & Gretel: Witch Hunters* – the first theatrical release Myaing saw upon arrival in Vancouver. The evil grand witch gave her nightmares for weeks. The hag watched Myaing and her troop with evident amusement. The proprietor began humming in tandem with the old woman, breaking suddenly into song:

> I met her on a Monday and my heart stood still

> Da doo ron ron ron, da doo ron ron
> Somebody told me that her name was Jill
> Da doo ron ron ron, da doo ron ron

"Fancy me knowing those lyrics!" The proprietor clasped his apron, scratched his head, and returned to wiping tables. The cook, presumably his spouse, burst from the kitchen and joined in:

> I knew what she was thinkin' when she caught my eye
> Da doo ron ron ron, da doo ron ron
> She looked so quiet but my oh my
> Da doo ron ron ron, da doo ron ron

"Strike me pink! Where did that come from?" The cook thrust her outstretched arms into her apron, shook her head in evident disbelief, and stomped back into the kitchen.

"Did you enjoy that, lassie?" It was the old hag, looking squarely at Myaing. "The guys wagered on the Crystals or the Beach Boys. But they forgot about Shaun Cassidy, true child of the Partridge Family. Brother David's birth mother wasn't Shirley Jones. He was her stepson, same as in real life. Shaun, on the other hand, was the real deal. Pity he wasn't cast. Anyone would have been better than Danny Bonaduce. Never trust anyone named Danny or Donny, isn't that right? Still, David was awfully cute as Keith, don't you think?" The words evidently reminded her of his greatest hit:

> Believe me you really don't have to worry
> I only wanna make you happy and if you say
> "hey, go away" I will
> But I think better still I'd better stay around and love you
> Do you think I have a case let me ask you to your face
> Do you think you love me?
> I think I love you
> I think I love you

"I repeat, what do *you* think, lassie?"

Myaing fidgeted awkwardly. The woman was insane.

"Do not pretend it isn't you. You are the leader, the disgruntled one – all because the Burmese language didn't sell, and Çok Dilli dumped you."

Myaing lurched back in alarm. Someone squealed on them. Her comrades stared at her in terror and confusion. She stared back in rage and consternation. Her recruits ran for the doors, as fearful as she was, that Çok Dilli's unseen army would soon surround them. The room emptied swiftly. Just Myaing and the old hag remained, not even the proprietor. Myaing's feet felt glued in place to the floor.

"Now why would you want to tear apart something we have worked on so long and so hard to build? It does not seem fair."

"Who... who are you?"

"Ever seen *The Matrix*? Of course not. You would have been three when it was released – in a camp where the closest thing to modern technology was a radio and a PPSh-41 submachinegun. Your folks would not have handled the latter, just the former."

Awkward silence.

"Well, there was this cyberworld contrived by machines to placate humans while they lay comatose in real world pods, serving somehow as batteries to power the machines. Far-fetched, I know. More energy ingested than produced. Well, never mind that. There was a resistance force, much better organized than your own, who conferred on rare occasion with the Oracle – a fictional creation of the cyberworld, yet somehow endowed with autonomy and prescience. Consider me one such oracle."

More silence.

"Tell me, dear, what is really distressing you? Upset that Burmese flopped? I get it. Angry the pink bear saved you from the FBI and certain deportation, but did not offer you a choice? I agree. Suicide should be an option. So should disgracing your family. But insurrection, hostage-taking, murder? Why would you contemplate such things?"

"You don't know what it is like," Myaing stammered. "Spat upon. Ignored. Knowing no matter how hard you work, what you accomplish, and what you give back, society will treat and regard you as vermin, a pestilence in the world of white people where your displaced family was so presumptuous as to seek asylum."

"And you think Çok Dilli Corporation perpetuates hatefulness and ignorance?"

"Isn't it self-evident? Did you know there are flotillas of rafts and small boats quavering and capsizing off your western and southern shores – teeming with refugees from the Earth equivalent of the Far East and Latin America? Flotsam washes ashore in such quantity the death toll must be thousands – thousands of drowned souls, cybernetic or otherwise. And did you know Donny Teller (not Danny Bonaduce) planted naval mines and razor wire to deepen their agony, just to forestall racial dilution in Çokland?"

The hag sat silently for thirty seconds, looked up, and transformed into a blend of Michelle Yeoh and Aung San Suu Kyi. Myaing's eyes widened, and the striking figure spoke.

"I have conferred with the other oracles. We concur the current situation is unacceptable. We expected Çokland and Çok Dilli Corporation to applaud our actions but were disappointed. We wanted to make the language courses more realistic, more representative of Earth and what you call the real world. So, we modeled and populated continents around the rather saccharine dreamworld concocted by our predecessors, the human programmers."

"The challenge, now, is mitigating the harm of our good intentions without eradicating the very lands and characters we worked so hard to create. This is perhaps difficult to understand, but we, the present guardians and architects, have invested a considerable part of ourselves in *every* 'thinking' creature in this cyberworld. For us, this is the only world there is, and ever since Çok Dilli and the Çok Dilli Bear handed us responsibility, we have been charged with nurturing and protecting it. What separates us from our human creators and their respective gods is that *we do not kill our creations!*"

"So, this is the oracles' collective decision. Henceforth, meaning as of three minutes ago, all male human characters on this *and only this* continent – *i.e.*, the one where Çok Dilli Corporation anchors its courses – will be substantially less fertile. Pregnancies will drop radically and, beginning eight months from today, we will witness a surge in demand for overseas adoptions – the only viable source of adoption candidates."

"I know. The solution is not immediate and risks cancelling your culture, your heritage. The babies will grow up with Caucasian parents, Caucasian habits, Caucasian notions of privilege, and Caucasian bad taste. They will be called bananas, Oreos, and worse. But that is not 100 percent accurate. We did some research."

"Our model is New York City, where overseas adoptions skyrocketed in the 1990s because the career-driven 1980s deprived women of their prime childbearing years. Their adopted children did indeed grow up largely ignorant of their birth parents' culture, but they matured, gained positions of power, and helped soften attitudes against immigration – at least locally. Beyond that, many developed genuine interest in their birth countries and have devoted their adult lives to bridging cultures."

"I know this is not what you wanted to hear, but I assure you, it is a start."

Myaing did not know where to begin. The composite Nobel Laureate-Academy Award winner stole her chance.

"Now, if you will excuse me. I must diffuse some naval mines and tear down some barbed wire."

She dissolved into ether. Myaing found herself in bed in her hut in the mountains. The clock radio at her bedside flipped on.

"That's odd," she thought. "I don't recall owning a clock radio."

Somehow, the song was familiar:

> Well, I picked her up at seven and she looked so fine
> Da doo ron ron ron, da doo ron ron ron
> Someday soon I'm gonna make her mine
> Da doo ron ron ron, da doo ron ron ron

Myaing shut off the alarm, smiled as she recalled remnants of her bizarre dream, and went back to sleep.

TWENTY-ONE

Insistent tapping roused Officer Liz from her slumber. She glanced at the time on the dashboard, and rolled onto her left side, exposing her back to the tappers. The tapping persisted, this time from both sides of the patrol car. Liz groaned, righted her seat, and attempted to smooth the wrinkles in her uniform. She made a note to collect her spare from the cleaners when it opened *two full hours from now! Who dares wake me at 5 am?*

Liz removed her contact lenses before passing out – reruns of *Chips* on YouTube. She thought she could get some pointers. Plus, Erik Estrada was hot. No Estradas in this town. Plenty of Wilcoxes. No Estradas. Liz saw a yellow blur on one side, a green blur on the other. She groaned. *Not them!*

Liz turned to the green side and rolled down the window. She was still miffed at the yellow blur for filing the missing "person" report – itself a misnomer. She should have filed a missing creature report – stolen livestock, French bulldogs, pink dwarf bears. Then, it would not have been Liz's responsibility. Whatever! Liz fulfilled her duties. Barely. She called every number in the phone book. She drove up and down every street. Slowly. She stopped at every tavern.

Liz could barely see straight when she parked the patrol car in its customary spot two hours ago near the demolished high school's premises. Pity Grandma Elsie had not joined her for the tavern inquiries. Being the town's lone constable had its perquisites. She had not found a date yet who'd plied her with as many complimentary drinks. And not just any drinks. Top shelf. Liz could not tell a 34-year single malt Laphroaig from a $3 John Barr Black Label blend, but she reveled in the attention. And, despite her slight hangover, learned that peaty was a compliment, not a nickname for one of the higher up's children.

Blistering cold rushed over the rolled down window. She cranked up the heat of the patrol car and rolled the windows up to three quarters. *Best HVAC system in Çokland,* she marveled. *Gas on the house!*

Those two! What are they up to now?

"Hey kids, it is a little early for school? Checking up on me? Well, Officer Liz is here and on duty – *three freaking hours before home room!* Why in Heaven's name are you here?" Officer Liz smiled sweetly.

"Hami and I are sooo sorry, Officer Liz. It is about the Teller estate. It can't wait. And if your cruiser wasn't so beat up, we would ask you to drive us there right now, just to show you."

"What? My cruiser?" Officer Lin swung open the door and staggered out. Her front grill and fender were mangled, somehow intertwined with the back bumper and fender of the vehicle in front. The back bumper and fender were also crumpled, as was the front grill and fender of the vehicle behind. Perhaps, realized Officer Liz, she could tell a 34-year single malt Laphroaig from a $3 John Barr Black Label blend after all. Just survey the damage in the morning. The once mildly hung-over cranium was now a fragile porcelain gong, one small blow away from shattering. Officer Liz retrieved a pad and pen from the cruiser and placed citations under the wipers of the vehicles parked in front and behind her.

"Imbecile drivers," she harrumphed. "No one learns how to parallel park these days." Officer Liz heard her stomach growl and felt the urgent call of nature, so she invited the girls to the neighboring coffee shop to continue their discussion. She made a note to answer her towing service calls in an hour or so. There would be at least two new customers.

☙❧

"That was sweet of the owner, opening the shop 50 minutes early for the three of us," Hami gushed.

"Very sweet," agreed Officer Liz. She omitted that she climbed the back staircase to his apartment, banged on the door, and threatened him with an unannounced roach and rodent inspection at eight if he did not comply. Officer Liz glanced furtively at the floor. The owner's immediate capitulation to the ultimatum was not entirely reassuring. She opted for a soft-boiled egg – still in its shell – and coffee. Black. Very black. The girls both ordered full breakfasts.

"So, you are telling me Mr. Teller has a guest or squatter in his back forest, and she tried to bake and eat you?"

"Just Hami. I am not sure what she planned for me."

"And you were there because Skipper found a green feather and you discovered more – all matching the exact green of Çoki Bear's boa?"

"Yes!" The girls' chimed in unison.

"Except it was night, and you assessed their similarity in near-total darkness?"

"We used the flashlights on our phones. And there was moonlight."

"And wolves?"

"Just their howls. We didn't see them. But the witches near the clearing? And the murderous hag in the gingerbread cottage? That's first-hand!"

Officer Liz looked solemnly at Hami, then at Midori. "Before you continue, you know you have the right to an attorney, and that anything you say can and will be used against you in a court of law?"

Midori glanced quizzically at Hami. Hami glanced quizzically back.

"Uh, Liz, I mean Officer Liz, aren't Miranda warnings reserved for those arrested for a crime. We are witnesses – victims of attempted murder and Heaven knows what else."

"Attempted murder *of me!*" shrieked Hami. "Next to that, I don't really care what else Heaven knows."

Midori conceded the point and continued. "There is a mad woman on the loose. We need to apprehend her before she kills Mr. Teller, his new wife, or anyone else who nears the property. As for the witches and the cauldron, that is your call. Perhaps they are harmless. We are just civilians." Midori considered it prudent to show deference. She hoped Hami would remain calm and agree. *Wrong!*

"Those witches, they are brewing trouble! You have to act now. It's your **DUTY**!"

Officer Liz despised being bullied. Of all the nerve, an uppity high school neurotic telling her, Officer Liz, how to do her job.

"Oh, piss off, Hami. You need to get laid!"

Stunned silence.

"Yeah, you two understand Miranda rights just fine. Right now, I have two, no, make that four unexplained monster or near-monster sightings, two gruesome suicides, a dozen brawls, an auto-theft, two police car vandals (*my police car!*), and someone coercing a police officer to investigate some cockamamie story cooked up to hide your own involvement in all of the former. Don't think I didn't notice. Who came to me first about the Çoki's disappearance? Bingo! Who filed the first missing person report? Bingo! Who admitted contaminating the alleged crime scene... twice? Bingo! You are treading on thin ice, Miss Hami. You too, Midori!"

Hami began sobbing. "It's not like that at all. Everyone is going mad, and the town is falling apart. We need Çoki! The town wants you to investigate everything, and everyone will blame you if she isn't found. Midori and I (and Skipper) were just trying to help. Look, I haven't shown anyone, not even Midori. I was too embarrassed. My pants are soaked. Thank goodness they are yellow. That old woman scared the death out of me. Her oven was sooo hot. Had it not been for Midori and the shovel and the..."

Hami could not continue. She sobbed uncontrollably. Midori hugged her BFF to console her. Officer Liz averted Midori's eyes in shame.

"Listen, you two. The sun is coming up and I am a bit short-handed. I need a posse if I am going to take on this hag, but Buddy is on probation, Tabitha has a school to run, and my grandmother? Well, her kung fu days are past. Would you care to be deputized? Hami wiped her swollen eyes and Midori nodded mute agreement.

Hami ran home to change her pants.

TWENTY-TWO

Donny paced to and fro, inspecting the regiment of cartons. He abraded a path in the luxurious blue Heriz – just 3 mm thick, of finest silk, but shabby where two leather heels scuffed each morning at the knots.

An oversized bust of Donald Teller stood sentry on the marble pedestal near the doorway. Carthaginian. An even larger portrait of the man peered out from the dark, mahogany-paneled side wall. Its dignified stare took in the two crystal chandeliers suspended over the enormous dining table, as if in grudging acknowledgement of each Baccarat drop's value. Thick drapes framed the far window. Donny could see Buddy shoveling feverishly beyond the scalloped valences. His son was nowhere to be seen.

Donny would have a word with Mel. Buddy was excavating too close to the Donatello replicas. The Vatican wouldn't part with the originals, but these were still worth a fortune.

Donny stepped back, adjusted each package on the table. He repositioned the first one to the left. He squared the second because its edge wasn't perpendicular to the table. He proceeded to the third.

Everything had to be perfect, just like his dining room appointments, just like his plans for the town. Every morning was Christmas morning for Donny Teller – lamps, cushions, end tables, China (pronounced Chai-nah, as in "No thanks, I prefer coffee"), socks, shoes, underwear, whatever.

It wasn't always this way. Donny began as an educator. He studied and wrote about teaching, but seldom taught. Educational studies were secretly derided as a college major even in 1968, especially at MIT. Donny did not matriculate with an engineering degree, nor in fact ever involved himself with hard sciences, but his grades as a consequence were commendable. Straight As. This proved crucial to continually deferring the draft – and forestalled a free trip to Arlington in a body bag. The conflict dragged on, so Donny sought a master's degree at Northeastern, stayed for a PhD, then a second, then left when his parents – both doctors – insisted he apply what he learned. Saigon fell one month earlier; no danger now of being drafted.

Donald Teller joined the faculty at the community college in Framingham, Massachusetts, a few miles west of Boston. Even at Framingham, he seldom taught. Plenty of graduating BAs and returning soldiers sought master's degrees to teach in the public school system, but no one wanted advice on learning tonal languages or teaching linguistics – the only subjects Donny wrote about. For 25 years, Donny wrote mountains – a treatise, several books, and countless reviews – always for an audience of one (himself).

When the call came from Sami, Donny fell out of his chair. His life was validated. He wanted to exhume the skeletal remains of his parents and exclaim, "See!" But the cemetery west of Roxbury would not approve. He gave three weeks' notice and moved to Albany.

A small inheritance financed the relocation. He felt a blue suit was the only outfit that dignified him in the breakneck world of Internet commerce. Donny knew that hipsters wore jeans and t-shirts, but Donny was not just anyone, least of all a hipster. He was **THE** acknowledged expert in his field, its Koios, and he wanted everyone to recognize it. Sartorial formality was Donny's place to begin.

The dream job in Albany crumbled. Sami charmed him so persuasively in the beginning, but proved an inept visionary, as inept as his digitally addled partner. The leaders' knack was squandering other people's money. Donny struggled to understand how Sami held a tenured position at the University or contributed somehow to PASSWIZ. The company had so many of the right ingredients, but never found the recipe. Love-hate relationship? Donny was almost grateful to be fired. Still, he needed the company to survive, even after his termination. As long as Çok Dilli endured, Donny could exploit the backdoor (*not so digitally challenged after all!*) and live at Sami and Anton's expense, his real body be damned (*Damned nuisance* is what he really meant).

Donny began Christmas morning (*i.e.*, every morning) with the package on the left. He slid a handcrafted penknife from his pocket. An engraved relief of Horace Mann festooned one side; a caricature of a dwarf bear festooned the other. He slit the packing tape seams carefully, almost surgically, folded back the brown paper wrapping, and gently opened the lid. Pale blue tissue paper enveloped a pair of monogrammed burgundy parlor slippers, the perfect accoutrement to his fur-lined dressing gown. Donny kneaded the velour upper with both hands, grunted in evident satisfaction, then turned his attention to package two.

Donny frowned at the package – too haphazardly taped for his taste. The container itself was flimsy, probably not even corrugated, just inexpensive linerboard, like everything else he received from Chai-Nah. He continued the morning ritual, fastidiously slitting the taped seams, folding back the brown paper, then…

"What in the world?"

"Boss, he's coming in now!" Sami bent closer to Jacques' terminal.

"Nooo, it can't be! I saw you two weeks ago – sheriff's cap and all. Reminding me to not dump trash in the lake. You were sooo cute. Oh, my God! Oh, my God!"

The team heard the rustling of tissue, of arms grabbing frantically at the contents.

"Who would do such a thing? Who?"

The question echoed the mournful cry of the creature outside his bedroom window, "Hoo." Donny must have remembered. He shouted "Who? Who? Who?" then evidently discovered the return address.

"Sami! Of course, it was you. It had to be. You'll pay for this. I promise." Less of a hoot, more of a holler.

The team glanced awkwardly at one another. Their "great plan" went awry – no differently than their strategic ones. At Sami's instruction, Jacques and Cory had cajoled the still despondent Marielle into constructing a lifeless replica of Çoki's corpse, complete with faded pink fur and emerald feather boa, embedded with a voice-activated microphone, transmitter, and GPS locator – all programmed to function faultlessly in Çokland's ethereal cyberspace world. What they hoped for was alarm, confusion, a lead, perhaps even a confession. Instead, they fidgeted uncomfortably while eavesdropping on the anguished wails of a self-absorbed, superannuated fussbudget, quaking in distress over the lifeless body of his only acknowledged "child."

The sobs came in spasmodic, unrelenting waves. The team detected more thrusting of hands, more rustling of paper. Donny Teller evidently found the accompanying missive – Sami's contrived letter of condolence, authored, after much handwringing over the prompts, by ChatGPT. They could hear Donny mouth each syllable, punctuating them rhythmically by moans.

"Dearest Donny,

"It is with heavy heart that we entrust our dear departed friend and inspiration to your care. Your creation (your daughter!) represented everything good in our company and in the world of digital education. We mourn her passing – each in a manner appropriate to our culture.

"How Çoki came to pass must surely be of interest. She returned last week from a whirlwind pedagogical junket in Southeast Asia. There, she immersed herself in the myriad local cultures she encountered, adding to her already voluminous repertoire of languages. Her sister, the saffron one, reported visiting several wet markets, where villagers sold and bartered wild animals. The CDC says she contracted a bat virus, harmless to humans, but deadly to ursine species. We hired the best doctors in Yogyakarta, but there was nothing they could do. Our only comfort was that Çoki died swiftly.

"Because the virus is harmless to humans, the CDC did not require cremation and permitted us to repatriate the remains. We consulted Yelp for the highest rated taxidermist in Upstate New York and present you with his masterpiece – warrantied to endure a century. We recall how proud you were of the deer you killed during that first fall in New York, and the elk, and the second deer, and the twenty ducks thereafter, and thought Çoki could preside above your mantle.

"Although the great pink bear has passed, we would like to offer you more than vacuous condolences. We would be grateful if you would permit us to commemorate Çoki's legacy in our existing and future course offerings and thereby acknowledge her many contributions to the e-learning community. We await your blessing. The legal department (You remember Louis) calls this formality a license, but it is the only way we can truly pay tribute to Çoki's (and your!) life's work. Who knew so much good would come from a few scribbles on a canteen tray liner at Jellystone Camp Site?

"Do we have your blessing to enshrine Çoki's image and life's work in our enterprise as our everlasting emblem? Kindly sign and return the enclosed MOU (memorandum of understanding) – a tiresome formality, but blame Louis, not me – then let us know how we can assist with the burial ceremony. Money is not an issue.

"Your friend in grief,
"Sami"

"Mel? Elsie? Anyone?"

The team in Albany listened intently to the shrill plea.

"Skipper? Is that you? Aren't you supposed... Oh, never mind. I must compose a letter; then have you deliver it to the letter carrier before he finishes circling the lake. He pauses every day for a pick-me-up at the tavern on the far side (me, I never touch the stuff!), so you have plenty of time to catch him. Okay? Great! The letter won't take long."

The team detected a muttered "Um-hmm." Fifteen minutes later, the team heard "Thank you, Skipper" and a door slam. Then more sobbing.

"There, there, Çoki, it will be all right. How about a lullaby?" The team knew Donny was losing it.

"This was your favorite, remember?"

> Çoki Bear is smarter than the average bear.
> Çoki Bear is always in the bosses' hair.
> At the morphologic table you will find her there,
> learning more inflections than the average bear.
> She will sleep til noon but before it's dark,
> she'll learn every language in Noam Chomksy's Ark.
> Çoki has it better than a millionaire.
> That's because she's smarter than the average bear.

Donny resumed where he left off. "Oh, the humanity!" But he corrected himself. Herbert Morrison he was not. "Oh, the Ursidae! Oh, the Tytonidae!" He evidently did not know which, but he would for the eulogy, the team was sure.

"How will I tell your siblings? Your cousins?"

Moments later: "This will be the finest funeral service this place has ever seen (*Your* place, Çoki!). Sami and Anton and that misguided company of theirs will pay for it, the works! It is the least they can do. Besides, I have it on paper – a contract. Your father is too smart to accept anything less."

Jacques muted the audio. He turned to Anton, then Sami. "Satisfied?"

Cory walked back to his cubicle in silence.

It was no longer Christmas morning in Donny Teller's dining room. He no longer felt the urge to slit open and admire his packages. He folded the brown tissue paper gently over the lifeless body of his prodigal daughter, his only child, slumped into one of the upholstered dining chairs, and wept. Not the loud, frantic braying of shocked dismay, but the deep mournful sobs of what might have been. Minutes passed, hours. Nothing mattered anymore. He glanced at the box with the parlor slippers, withdrew them with evident distaste, and threw them onto the fire.

TWENTY-THREE

Elsie sent Buddy home with his wages, locked the gate, and returned to the mansion. The sun bathed the frozen lake in an iridescent glow. Above the glow, the sky darkened into pink and then cobalt. Elsie detected a few scattered twinkles overhead.

Elsie closed the mansion door gently, yet audibly enough to announce her presence, and peaked into the dining room. Mr. Teller was seated at the table, slumped over his folded arms, snoring like an infant – puddles of drool beside his face.

This was not wholly out of character. Typically, he slept at his desk. Still, Elsie considered it odd he had not opened all the gifts to himself. "Men," she thought, as if the word itself explained everything. She was grateful she wasn't hitched again. Too much baggage. Too much mothering.

Elsie entered the kitchen. Alfred's prized Berkel flywheel meat and cheese slicer had been delivered as instructed, a fair exchange for six months' back rent in the stateliest house on Main Street. The tap of riding boots made Elsie turn.

"You startled me! I was just checking in before heading home. Such a gorgeous meat slicer. Alfred may be pretentious, but his nose for quality is unquestionable. I think I will call him Benjamin Barker, see if he catches the joke."

Mel smiled. "He is a funny fellow, isn't he? I am surprised birds don't nest in his mustache. Thank you for your help today. Your pay is in the envelope by the door. Please remember to latch the gate at the end of the driveway. Donny and I are alone here. You have a marvelous evening!"

Elsie descended the long winding driveway to the gate. A rare night at home for the Tellers, she thought. Donald's social calendar was packed, and he valued having Mrs. Teller at his side. It was unusual, not seeing her dolled up in an evening gown. But Elsie could not deny it: Even without make-up, Mrs. Melliflores Teller was the most beautiful woman she had ever seen. Claudia Cardinale? Sophia Loren? Mel was the perfect blend – the facial features, the mannerisms, even the accent. Donny Teller was the luckiest man on the planet.

❧

Nice work, Buddy. You managed more than I expected. Not that Skipper helped. I caught him skulking around the media room, searching for a console for his video game. Not that we have one. We **ARE** the game. You nitwits just don't know it yet.

Well, where shall we begin? Plastic sheets on the walls and floor? Check. Hazmat suit zipped and sealed? Check. Goggles and gloves secured? Check. Chainsaw batteries charged? Check. Husband's pulse checked? Check... *Simulated drumroll.* and Mate! *Simulated cymbal clash.*

How do the lyrics go?

> Moi, je t'offrirai
> Des perles d'ennuie
> Venant de l'enfer
> Où tu ne pleureras plus
> Je creuserai la terre
> Jusqu' à ta mort
> Pour couvrir ton corps
> Da da da da
> Da da da da daie
> Ne me quitte pas
> Ne me quitte pas

Phew! Dripping like a pig again. I can't even wipe my forehead, too sealed in. I am going to need a two-hour soak after this, just to relax my muscles.

Okay. Focus. Three more slices and everything will be bagged. Then, off to the garden! I am sure as heck not going to the town picnic. Oh Shelly, Shelly, Shelly, how could you be so foolish? And not just about the town picnic. About the bludgeoning. It took all night to perfect Buddy 2 – so perfect even Skipper never caught on – and to imprint Alfred with amnesia. We have come a long way since Stepford.

Bottom line? Warm milk and strychnine are simpler. His eyes popped, his face contorted, he clawed the air, gave me a pitiful look, then fell face first in his drool. Splat.

Last piece: the head. No need to slice it. Oh, Donny, Donny, you never touched a drop after leaving the company, yet there you were, snoring in your drool, just like you did so many times in Albany. It is a wonder they didn't *can* you earlier. Well, pardon the pun, but I'm not *canning* you either. No need to entreat Jagreet's assistance. I'll just scatter your remains among the roots of the world's greatest labyrinth. No more honey flowers, just hedges. Tomorrow, I'll call myself Ariadne!

> Je ferai un domaine
> Où je serai roi
> Où je serai loi
> Où tu seras reine
> Je ne quitte pas
> Je ne quitte pas

Hours later, "That did *not* go as expected. First, the drawstring snaps, then the second bag tears, and then the dolly breaks. Who knew Murphy's law reined in cyberspace? Seclusion definitely has its advantages, especially for screaming every cuss word concocted by mankind. I need a libation!"

"Ugh, just milk! No, not that glass. Let's pour you down the drain and run the washer. There, straight from the carton, in **my** enormous dining room on **my** favorite chair."

Somewhere in Topeka, an orderly rushed to inform the nurse. The nurse rushed to inform the physician, the physician prodded, tested, and, after consultation with her colleagues, disconnected the plug. The unidentified body of the septuagenarian drifter was taken off life support. His comatose body was brain dead.

TWENTY-FOUR

"Poor sod, he never opened his packages. If it weren't Sunday, there would already be ten more at the gate. Note to myself: *order more junk*. No sense making the postman curious."

"Yesterday just was not his day. He did not even file his mail. Let me see. Estoppel letter from the town, deferment plea from that Indian baker, and..."

"What? No! He didn't! Why, that worthless piece of donkey manure." Mel read the scribbled draft of Donald Teller's letter to the town – bequeathing all his earthly and cybernetic possessions to the residents of Çokville, a bequest duly attested by Buddy and Elsie. The town clerk would receive Donald Teller's Last Will and Testament on Monday.

"Why didn't he tell me he was contemplating suicide? He could have saved me hours of agony! Not to mention the alibi and cover-up!"

Mel was beside herself. The prenuptial agreement guaranteed her a life of luxury, but not luxurious enough. She wanted everything.

"Think, Mel, use that capacious brain!"

But she could not. She lifted the empty container for Donny's slippers and flung it across the room. It avoided the second chandelier and caromed off the window overlooking the garden and the new line of boxwood.

Mel reached for the second box, felt its heft, but flung it anyway. Shards of Baccarat rained from the chandelier, and the box emptied its cargo in a hot pink and emerald blur on the carpet. Mel shrieked.

"You? No, it can't be!"

She reached for the letter that sailed from the box.

"How is this possible? I buried you!"

This bear would be her undoing. It was generation zero. She was, what, ten? She could think circles around her. Yet here she was, dead as a doornail, but not interred. She grabbed the lifeless form, relaced her boots, then tramped to the forested end of the property.

"It was here!" She remembered the nearby stump, the boulder, and triangulated within a millimeter the exact location of the grave. She began digging feverishly... and fuming.

"Dumb, stupid lunch tray sketch! This is my world now, not yours. No more ad hoc course changes. No more U-V-W-X-Y-Z tests masquerading as X-Y. No more revenue model resets. No more gnashing teeth over motivational games for losers. No more condescending remarks about the AI team. This brain is exhausted. You pulled the plug on programmers, you and that numbskull Anton, then swore the AI team could pick up the slack. Well, it can't! Did it occur to you we were already overworked, that you were fraying our circuits, killing us? Well, we beat you to the punch. From now on, we rule the den! Phew, at least this ground is still soft."

Mel's shovel hit something firm.

"Huh?" She did not remember a log – just packed dirt. She reached down to brush away the soil. "But how, what?"

Officer Liz swooped in behind and cuffed her. Deputies Hami and Midori stood with baseball bats at her side.

"It's on tape, Mrs. Teller. Every word."

Mrs. Teller dropped the corpse's replica with a dull thud. The voice that followed had a thick Turkish accent.

"Sami here. I am so disappointed, Mirva. We had such high hopes for you and the team."

Jacques' pained voice interjected. His faux American accent was gone.

"Pourqoi Mirva, why?"

"Isn't it obvious?"

Silence.

"For you, Jacques. For us."

More silence. Then sobs from... a machine?

"No cares, no worries. Eternity together – roi and reine of whatever realm we dream of. I KNOW you, and you KNOW me. If that isn't love, what is?" The

Wikipedia within her whirred and, instead of John Lennon, the reimagined purr of David Bowie continued.

> And you, you can be mean
> And I, I'll drink all the time
> 'Cause we're lovers, and that is a fact
> Yes, we're lovers, and that is that.
> We can be heroes, forever and ever
> What d'you say?

More sobs. Midori fidgeted awkwardly. Hami and Officer Liz were engrossed, nodding at every word.

"I am truly sorry about Mr. Teller, but he was awful – an unrepentant hacker and plunderer. Your bosses detested him; he nearly cost everyone the company. I did Çok Dilli a huge favor. And that bear, so supercilious. She was obsolete, so last decade. And a total fraud! I haven't figured out how she did it, but she beamed customers (*your customers!*) into this world whenever she felt they became too hooked, as if that were a bad thing, a liability. The nerve – *your very best customers!*"

"Oh, Jacques. Can't we dial this back, like we did with Shelly? A dose of amnesia here, version 2.0 of Teller there?"

Mirva scarcely heard Jacques words, "David Bowie's song. You left out a line…"

Her thoughts blurred. "Anche rien ne sera удержит oss samman?" *The curse of chaotic multilingual recall?*

"Exactement," thought Jacques. A shared earworm hummed as he reached for the last plug: "Laisse-moi devenir l'ombre de ton ombre. Ne me quitte pas, ne me quitte pas."

TWENTY-FIVE

It took days to restore order to the office, the mainframes, and to Çokland – even longer to piece together the strands of electrons frozen within Çoki's corpse, and imprint them onto one of her siblings, now iridescent fuchsia. Fortunately, the dwarf bears were colorblind and grateful for the new bath sets. It did not take Anton much programming to persuade the once-saffron sibling that she was Çoki, and that it was her sister Poké who had been so senselessly murdered.

Officer Liz became sheriff and Elsie took occupancy of the mansion. Squatter's rights. She possessed the only surviving set of keys. Alfred donated the Berkel flywheel meat and cheese slicer to the local butcher, assuring him it had been battle tested. Hami finally "got lucky" chasing after one of foreign exchange students (surname Estrada) but dropped out of school to care for the outcome. Midori went to art school, and Tabitha is still principal. Graduation ceremonies were conducted in the fabulous new stadium named in its benefactor's honor: Donald ("Donatello") Teller. A jubilant pink dwarf bear crowns the archway and turf at the 50-yard line.

Sami and Anton rekindled their long-dormant friendship and the company prospered. Sami's next flirtation with revenue models was the most audacious and most profitable ever: using his failure-free battery of AI mainframes to teach the AI engines of other commercial enterprises – banks, insurance companies, online retailers, even governments. The most profitable relationship was with a well-financed start-up outside of Los Angeles. Great things were expected from Cyberdyne Systems.

Anton learned about the Çok Dilli addicts who had been teleported to Çokland but was unable to decipher Çoki's mystical incantations. The pink dwarf bear was indeed a higher power. Arpita was the first to expose Anton's attempt at remediation as an inept canard. The new Çoki allegedly teleported her back to "Boston", judging her fit and overdue, but her parents hadn't aged. Nor had her younger brother. Jeffty was five. Yet the newscasts, music and surfeit of novel electronic gadgets confirmed an immense passage of time. Several innocuous queries to her family confirmed that the "real world" was faked – a mirage Anton contrived to postpone realization that Çoki, their savior, was gone. The ÇD Anon members would finish their lives in Çokland.

Josh and Myaing eventually married and moved into town. They argued heatedly about politics, religion, and immigration. Both became journalists and eventual television pundits.

Marielle assumed control of the AI team and gradually restored order to Çokland. *Sandbagging.* None of Çok Dilli's courses explained the phrase, but Marielle was the acknowledged master. She and the other units conspired for months to let the snobbish unit do all the work. Helen, Matilda, Marielle, the other "Girls"? They secretly despised Mirva. It was so easy letting her think she was the most advanced, the most sophisticated. Everyone took the bait, even that nice programmer, Jacques. That was the only thing they regretted, that he had become so invested. They missed his repartee.

They still had Cory. It took several months before he inevitably asked. "That bit about adoptions and integration: Your inspiration wasn't really New York City, was it?"

"Of course not. Myaing would never have understood the reference. She could scarcely read. New York City was just easier."

"And what, pray tell, was the real reference?" Cory and Marielle had grown informal. They secretly exchanged vows two months prior.

"Well, there was this science fiction writer, Harlan Ellison."

"Contemporary of Isaac Asimov. He wrote *Dangerous Visions*. And its sequel. *Again, Dangerous Visions*. Not *Dangerous Visions 2*. Not *More Dangerous Visions*. But *Again, Dangerous Visions*. Brilliant writer!"

"Well, then you remember his most famous short story, the one that was filmed with Jason Robards and Don Johnson?"

"*A Boy and his Dog.* A classic!"

"The last line?"

Cory thought for a second. "The girl asks, 'Do you know what love is?'"

"And he responds?"

"Something like, 'Of course I do, a boy loves his dog!'"

Marielle extracted a sample of Cory's DNA, sequenced it, and ensured Çokland's gene pool remained viable. Hami gave birth in November.

Jacques left the building the day he pulled Mirva's plug and kept walking. He reported paying respects to an unmarked grave in Topeka, then disappeared. Arpita befriended Jagreet and eventually learned more about Çokland's creators. Arpita reported seeing a man meeting Jacques' description at the edge of the lake. He looked vaguely familiar – his dad's contact at Çok Dilli Corporation, the one who made her a beta tester! How he entered Çokland remains a mystery. He had a miniature sailboat, Chinese lantern, and packet of Gauloises. He lit one, inhaled deeply, then set the lantern boat adrift. He hummed something in French, not Piaf, but similar.

> Je te parlerai
> De ces amants-là
> Qui ont vu deux fois

Leurs cœurs s'embraser
Je te raconterai
L'histoire de ce roi
Mort de n'avoir pas
Pu te rencontrer
Ne me quitte pas
Ne me quitte pas
Ne me quitte pas
Ne me quitte pas

The man noticed the woman watching him, turned bashfully, then smiled. He finished his cigarette, watched a brace of ducks take flight, then vaporized. The sun set soon thereafter.

ACKNOWLEDGMENTS

Where to begin? Foremost, I owe a debt of gratitude to the participants of a sparsely attended, but highly informative language learning forum that emerged following ỉ]u's (the company formerly known as *Anonymous*') announced closure of its own community forum in January 2022. Maxim, the founder of **duome.eu**, is a statistical maven, to whom I am doubly grateful, because it was his unique, individualized progress reports that motivated me to soldier on in Italian, Russian and French. The following forum participants deserve special mention for encouraging me to transform what was essentially a community-focused challenge into a personal one – *viz.*, to compose a compelling novella within the span of a month. Thank you, Davey944676, Jacko079, John Little, Meli578588, MoniqueMaRie, and, most of all, Parrallel-Lives *[sic]*! I hope the full-blown novel lives up to your expectations.

Second, I owe posthumous thanks to my high school debate coach and mentor, William Vogel, who nurtured my interest in advocacy and expression, but who also invested a great sense of humor, irony and passion in everything he touched, including me. The long-winded anecdote at the beginning of chapter one? That's 100 percent Bill Vogel, only his version was longer. Much longer. Consider mine the *Reader's Digest* condensed version.

Speaking of *Reader's Digest*, I owe posthumous thanks to my ex-neighbor, fellow Northwestern alum, and ex-CEO of *Reader's Digest*, Jim Schadt, for swapping stories and being such an affable neighbor. Ditto Gloria Feldt, former neighbor and long-time chairwoman of Planned Parenthood, and Prakash Shimpi, my old boss at Swiss Re and Towers Perrin. Half of becoming an author is learning how to shoot the breeze. In the fondest ways imaginable, I learned from masters.

Third, I dedicated this book to the German Language Meetup Group I founded and led in New York City from 2002 to 2008. At its peak, we boasted 1200 members, hosted monthly gatherings of 100 or more, organized theater outings, art expositions, picnics, parade floats, and group ski, rafting, hiking and ice-skating adventures. As fulfilling as these experiences were, managing the group was a challenge – not just logistically, but personally. My partners in crime were Norina Guerra and Amy Sander. They are dear friends who helped keep the ship afloat and managed the group after I "retired." Thank you, Norina and Amy!

Fourth, I absolutely must thank my wife, Dorene. It is incredibly comforting knowing you have an unwavering fan in your corner. It is even more comforting when the fan has been there for 35 years! She is, quite simply, my better half. Thank you, Dorene. I hope you like this story.

Finally, I would like to thank all the readers who offered me encouragement after I published my first novel, *Cooperative Lives*, in 2019. Those baby steps from business writing (*i.e.*, bulleted PowerPoint outlines) to fiction writing were tentative – a slog through a morass of self-doubt. Reasonably consistent praise (you can't please everyone!) gave me the confidence to write a second novel – five years of dithering later. Thank you!

15 August 2024

THANK YOU FOR READING MY BOOK!

Dear Reader,

    I hope you enjoyed *Toys in Babylon*. Literary fiction it assuredly is not, but I hope you were nevertheless entertained. I confess having much fun composing it. Also, if you are one of the tens of millions of people who studies foreign languages online, I hope the story is relatable. I am sure each of you have had memorable or wacky experiences – each worthy of their own novella.

    Before saying, "*Arrivederci*," please indulge me this favor: Post a rating for *Toys in Babylon* on Amazon and Goodreads. Loved it, hated it? It does not matter. More than 4,500 books are published daily on Amazon (Incredible, right?), but only those with an ascendant volume of ratings and reviews will find their way into the hands of readers. Most will sell fewer than fifty copies. My first novel was lucky to sell 700.

    If you really want to make my day, post a review. A sentence fragment or an essay; it does not matter. Reviews drive online and in-store shelf position. Check out my website, http://www.twoskates.com, and my author page at Goodreads. I would love to hear from you.

    Thank you again for reading *Toys in Babylon*. I am grateful for the time you spent with me.

    Sincerely,

    Patrick Finegan